THE INHERITORS

THE INHERITORS

A Novel

by Philip Atlee

With an introduction by E. R. Bills

With a foreword by Liam Phillips

TCU PRESS
Fort Worth, Texas

First Published by Dial Press in 1940
Republished by TCU Press in 2026

Library of Congress Cataloging-in-Publication Data

Names: Atlee, Philip, 1915-1991 author | Bills, E. R. writer of introduction
Title: The inheritors : a novel / by Philip Atlee ; with an introduction by E.R. Bills.
Description: Fort Worth : TCU Press, [2026] | "COPYRIGHT © 1940, 2026 BY PHILIP ATLEE."--ECIP title page verso. | Includes bibliographical references.
Identifiers: LCCN 2026019856 | ISBN 9780875659695 paperback
Subjects: LCSH: Heirs--Texas--Fort Worth | Children of the rich | Wealth--Moral and ethical aspects | Fort Worth (Tex.)--Social life and customs | LCGFT: Novels | Satirical fiction
Classification: LCC PS3501.T56 I54 2026
LC record available at https://lccn.loc.gov/2026019856

TCU PRESS

TCU Box 298300
Fort Worth, Texas 76129
www.tcupress.com

This book is
dedicated to
Lorraine Sherley,
who was a light in
darkness . . .

Introduction

A. C. Greene's *The Fifty Best Books on Texas*, first published in 1981, is an important survey of essential books about our state, including fiction, nonfiction, historical, cultural, and classic titles. Greene revised the survey in 1998, retitling it *The 50+ Best Books on Texas.* He removed a few books and added several more, but *The Inheritors* made both cuts.

I always found this interesting, mainly because it was the only title of the original fifty, or later 50+, that was virtually made to disappear upon publication. In fact, I was somewhat surprised Greene had ever even heard of it. But I'm glad he had, and I also appreciate the intriguing anecdote he relates about Philip Atlee, who we now know as Fort Worth native James Young Phillips: "When I included this long-neglected work in my original listing of fifty best, the author wrote me an amused note, insisting, 'Quit stomping on an old man's grave!'"

I don't know whether Phillips was amused or bemused. But that's why we're here.

In Texas, the book appears to have been panned all around. Everywhere outside of Texas, however, reviewers took note. Before *The Inheritors* was released, the June 15, 1940, Kirkus review of the work was encouraging: "This is a book that will appeal to those who started on [F. Scott] Fitzgerald and followed through to [John] O'Hara [author of *Appointment in Samarra* and *BUtterfield 8*], and who demand the best in that particular genre. It is even tougher than O'Hara; there's some of Caine's sadistic side [James Caine, author of *The Postman Always Rings Twice* and *Double Indemnity*]; it is a full-blooded job, written in a virile, vital prose style which makes a terrific impact."

The December 1, 1940, edition of *The Baltimore Sun* called the book "unadorned and powerful and reminiscent of James Caine and the early Hemingway." The December 23, 1940, edition of *The New Republic* said the author "writes of the younger Country Club set around Fort Worth with a freshness and ease of a natural talent on the loose," and the story "has the vitality and conviction of a scandal whispered in the cloakroom about the merrymakers you can glimpse in the ballroom beyond." The January 19, 1941, review in the *Pittsburgh Press* called Atlee's George Jimble "a rich man's Studs Lonigan" and issued a warning: "There is danger of taking a book like this too seriously. There is a greater danger in not taking it seriously enough. . . . There's some very fine writing to be found."

A couple of years later, when George Sessions Perry—National Book Award–winning American novelist, World War II correspondent, and one of the highest paid magazine contributors of the day—curated *Roundup Time: A Collection of Southwestern Writers*, he included excerpts from *The Inheritors* alongside those of John Steinbeck's *The Grapes of Wrath* (1939) and Oliver La Farge's *Laughing Boy* (1929). *Laughing Boy* earned La Farge a Pulitzer Prize in 1930. *The Grapes of Wrath* won the National Book Award, earned Steinbeck a Pulitzer Prize, and figured prominently in his 1962 Nobel Prize in Literature.

Later, some critics suggested *The Inheritors* was an edgier, adult version of *The Catcher in the Rye* a decade before J. D. Salinger's adolescent classic appeared. *The Catcher in the Rye* is considered an American classic and one of the best English-language novels of the twentieth century.

Greene, himself, suggested that *The Inheritors* was written "thirty or forty years before its time," and there's the rub. Except, initially, it wasn't a rub. It was a crushing blow.

Imagine yourself an aspiring writer, surely having read Hemingway, Fitzgerald, and Steinbeck, and maybe even O'Hara, Caine, Farrell, and La Farge. Now picture yourself beginning to be compared to or enjoying the curated company of these American literary giants in your mid-twenties.

Caine was forty-two when *The Postman Always Rings Twice* was published. Steinbeck was thirty-seven when *The Grapes of Wrath* was published. Salinger was thirty-two when *The Catcher in the Rye* was published. Farrell was twenty-eight when *Young Lonigan* was published. La Farge was twenty-eight when *Laughing Boy* was published. Fitzgerald was twenty-eight when *The Great Gatsby* was published. Hemingway was twenty-seven when his "early" *The Sun Also Rises* was published.

I'm not a numbers guy, but one number jumps out at me in any discussion of *The Inheritors*. James Young Phillips was twenty-five when the book was published.

Twenty-five.

And, though presumably having had the benefit of reading several of the aforementioned American literary giants and the works that made lasting marks in American letters, Phillips's mark—which seems to have verged on the prodigious—was summarily dismissed, condemned, and erased.

Imagine that for a moment.

Now, picture it as an aspiring writer.

Consider the immediate and long-term implications.

•••

James Young Phillips was born on January 8, 1915, in Fort Worth. Phillips's father, a prominent member of a major law firm, represented members of the River Crest Country Club's big oil families, helping make the family quite well off; he was also a director of a local bank and president of the prestigious Fort Worth Club. He was well-connected, and the family enjoyed a mansion right off one of the greens of the exclusive River Crest Country Club golf course. James and his three brothers led a charmed existence until his father succumbed to pneumonia in the late summer of 1928.

The elder Phillips's affairs were in order, but the 1929 stock market crash wiped out the family's fortune. Practically destitute, James's mother sold what she could from their big house and went to work for the Fort Worth Independent School District. She and her sons were suddenly poor in a stately home located in one of the wealthiest neighborhoods in the nation.

This turn of events no doubt shaped how James Young Phillips and "Philip Atlee" would come to view what is referred to in *The Inheritors* as the "dollar aristocracy," but it doesn't diminish the power or the acuity of the perspective. Phillips may have melodramatically envisioned himself a "Threadbare Galahad" (one of the original working titles for this book), but the pages evidence the virility of a Hemingway, the poetic sense of Fitzgerald, and the intellectual vitality of a Steinbeck.

In some obvious ways, *The Inheritors* is a book for its times; but in other, profound ways, it is a book for all times. There is no question the "dollar aristocracy" has done a lot for Fort Worth and the arts in general, but it was a towering mistake to exile Phillips's intense 1940 testament. It arguably killed a part of the author and robbed an untold number of Texans and Americans of the author's literary prospects and promise.

Until now.

The Inheritors is as relevant as ever.

E. R. Bills

March 27, 2026

Foreword

Inheritance: A Son's Perspective

As the sole legal heir of my father's body of written works, I can only write about *The Inheritors* as a man who came to the slow realization that he was the owner of something missing. It certainly fits the relative definition of a "lost book," lingering in legend and all but nonexistent with the exception of expensive out-of-print original copies very seldomly surfacing at auction houses and rare booksellers. Indeed, *The Inheritors*, a raw and reckless appraisal of the elite class and socialite scene surrounding the River Crest County Club in Fort Worth, Texas, and the outrage that followed its publication was only a piece of family folklore for me as well. The novel was barely mentioned during the twenty-one years I lived with my father and mother, and I didn't see or have in my possession a copy of the book until after my father's passing in 1991 when I was gifted one by Olcott, his sole remaining brother, on November 3, 1992—as he dutifully inscribed on the interior.

I'm of the opinion that my father—James Young Phillips (a.k.a. Philip Atlee)—lived two lives. In his first he had all the remarkable adventures he describes in his memoir, *No Fixed Abode*, a rambling recollection of his privileged youth growing up on the prestigious River Crest neighborhood, up through his young adulthood, and into his middleage. Though Jim Phillips was indeed born with a silver spoon in his mouth, I think he was forever shocked into a troubling realization of mortality at only thirteen years of age by his own father's sudden and untimely death from pneumonia in 1928 at age thirty-seven. Everything that followed was somewhat bittersweet, and probably more the former than the latter.

In his memoir, Jim briefly recounts the writing of *The Inheritors*, the drama and dysfunction of World War Two and his role in it, glamour-filled Broadway nights under the employ of showman Billy Rose, writing screenplays for Hollywood superstars, and penning his numerous books of spy fiction. But how telling is it that at the end of his own life, when he writes his autobiography, he cannot once bring himself to mention his first wife's real name in the text? It's not an oversight. So unabashedly, wholly enamored was the man—and so deeply wounded at losing the love of his life—that he can only refer to her by the touching and timeless pet name, "Zen."

For the record, her name was Joyce Phillips, née Clayton, and she was also the mother to my father's firstborn son, Shawn. From what I know, following the outrage over *The Inheritors*, my father was further gutted by the failure of his marriage to Joyce, the dissolution of their little family, and the horrific experience of watching her waste away from an incurable illness, Raynaud's disease. It was a cruel turn of fate which ultimately ended with her repeated attempts, and eventual success, at suicide by overdose in 1956. Jim Phillips was an oddly sentimental man and sincerely loving in his remote way, but he was incapable of escaping the cynicism and bitterness that life had dealt him—all of which contributes to *The Inheritors* absence from print or public awareness for the last eighty-six years. He left it all behind intentionally, without looking back.

My father's second life began at fifty when I was born in 1964, long after he had permanently fled the Fort Worth scene, having essentially abandoned my brother Shawn, and he simply started another family from scratch without any meaningful connections to his brothers or his first son. Upon my initial reading of my father's memoir at twenty-four, it was a profoundly disorienting experience to realize that I wasn't even aware of the majority of the people he mentions. It was akin to being introduced to an entirely different man than the one I had grown up with and loved as my father, albeit one eerily similar in features and disposition, though possessed of a wholly different mindset and dynamic projection of personal confidence. That remarkable man had exited the scene long before I showed up. It's as if I grew up with his ghost.

You see, the world of *The Inheritors* and its characters—the individuals on whom they're based and the real people and places which defined my father's first life—are themselves mostly legend and lore to me. Those people and that social-emotional territory are from a different life and timeline, all but hermetically sealed off from my and my mother's experience of Jim Phillips. I didn't meet my brother Shawn until I was fifteen and he was thirty-six. I met two of my father's three brothers, Edwin and David, only twice, and his brother Olcott only four times in total.

Further, and to my own astonishment, when I queried Shawn for the writing of this preface, he stated flatly that *The Inheritors*, published in 1940, three years before his birth, was never mentioned in any detail during his life with Jim and Joyce. As Shawn lived with my father until his early teens, this seemed to indicate to me that the flashpoint of scandal surrounding the book had been so intense and pervasive that the book had been all but completely wiped from the memories of both the people and the community which it portrayed, and rendered "unmentionable" to everyone even remotely affiliated with the work. It's as if it only existed for a brief moment and then vanished completely—from bookstores, from libraries, from resellers. It was just gone.

As far as *The Inheritors* is concerned, the Phillips family seemed to be perfectly content for it to be relegated to obscurity. Fifty years after the publication, Olcott and his wife Polly—who, in 1992, yet resided in the affluent-but-aging River Crest enclave—were still talking about it more with regret for the impact than praise for the author, though they did seem to hold it as a point of pride that they had been so closely associated with such a spark of infamy. From my vantage, their proximity had permanently limited their perspective. I never trucked with the idea that the book should remain obscure just because it had ended up that way.

As with my brother, my father didn't speak about *The Inheritors* at any length during my time with him. But while I certainly don't believe for a moment that he was ashamed of it, I was acutely aware that *they* had been—his family, friends, and associates. It was only after my father's passing, on that aforementioned occasion when Olcott presented me with my only copy of the book, that my mother and I learned of the true size and nature of the genuine controversy and scandal that ensued. Seated in Olcott's elegant living room, it was shocking to us then to hear of the rumors that the family and affronted associates had scoured Fort Worth and the surrounding towns, buying every copy of the book they could find and summarily destroying them in hopes of limiting the local damage. It is still shocking to me to this day that no one in my family who was alive at that time ever denied that it happened.

I believe that behind Jim's reluctance to maintain closer relationships with his family was resentment for the way that they treated him after the book's publication. Yes, speculation on my part, but perhaps the more accurate given my experience of growing up with him in his self-imposed isolation. He was run out of town on a metaphorical rail, and rather than ever seek reconciliation, he chose to literally wander the world until he found other people more to his liking to settle down with. Who can blame him?

I knew both Jim Phillips, my father, and Philip Atlee, the author, and they were both but part and parcel of one troubled man. He was a semifunctional alcoholic who participated in my life to the degree that his addiction allowed. Shawn and I always saw through his gruff exterior to the stoic, funny, emotionally conflicted, and deeply sensitive man he was underneath, and we loved him dearly for all of it and always will. While my father's subsequent works of espionage fiction paid for certain aspects of my life, I believe he grew tired of them—the rote process of churning them out, and what they represented of his efforts compared to what he originally intended to do with his writing. *The Inheritors*, of course, is an ironic title for me, because by the time I had the opportunity to read it at twenty-seven, my father had passed away and I had inherited the book itself. Like everyone else who's read it, I wondered what could have been.

I can think of no other modern novel so utterly forgotten and abandoned that in retrospect is now considered a legitimate American classic. *The Inheritors* and its author were both victims of a very real "cancel culture," which existed long before said term was coined; but what greater testament to its relevance and legitimacy could there be than the fact that, despite the efforts of those portrayed in the book, those closest to its author and his family, and the outraged community at large, the book has persisted and now returns like a phoenix—no doubt to their infinite vexation if they knew. Jim Phillips had a hearty laugh, and he would let loose a great one out of this.

Though it's well known that the characters in *The Inheritors* are thinly veiled portraits of then-extant prominent individuals, the actual players in my father's funny, brutal *roman á clef* have long since left the stage; only their masks remain to act the parts that he so cleverly crafted for them from their own foibles.

As per his wishes, my father donated his body to science. After his death there was no funeral, no remembrance, no gravestone. He, like this book, was simply here and then gone. It is with pride, joy, and my eternal gratitude that Philip Atlee has now come full circle back to his alma mater with TCU Press's republication of his greatest work. Enjoy.

Liam Phillips
Los Angeles, 2026

Preface

THIS is no golden legend. Instead, it is a bare, transcripted tale of youth. A guy named Mumford spilled a little blood on the story, and all of us helped the action along, but there was no great bravery involved. It all happened in Fort Worth, Texas, but that was only an accident of narration. The story could have been told anywhere in America, about any place that had a country club. Let no one think that the group herein described was atypical of youth. We were only a fringe, but there were a few of us everywhere. Many of our contemporaries, in the middle thirties of the twentieth century, led admirably sane lives and had a brisk Y.M.C.A. outlook. These are the ones who will undoubtedly save the country when the going gets toughest, but, as Cavin Jarvis said, they were damned uninteresting. I suppose the formation of character is a tedious thing.

My name is George Bellamy Jimble, the 3d, and this is a story about me and some friends of mine. To be proper, a story must have a hero, but it is a trifle difficult to pick out a hero in this one. I suppose you could just call me a decadent Tom Sawyer, and let it go at that. Cavin Jarvis could qualify as a chromium-plated Huck Finn, and Fred Bradley might be old Jim, the slave. None of us was older than twenty-five, none younger than eighteen, and we were a rebellious part of an established American pattern.

To understand the story, you must know something of our background. Fort Worth is a town sprawling without design over the Texas uplands, a town disfiguring three gentle rivers and a hill. The time was 1935, a.d. The terrain was rolling, and roads led into the town from fifteen ways. The soil was good for crops, and the air was clean. In the town's center, a handful of buildings bulked against the sky, and from them, as spokes from a hub, rolled out streets of smaller buildings. These blended into residential districts until finally there were only unsightly shacks, tourist camps, and filling stations littering the prairie edge. To the west and north, the land swelled away toward the staked plains. From these plains came cattle, by truck and train, to be sledged on the head and packed at the plants north of town. Toward Louisiana and the Gulf, the land waved toward the scrubby pine of East Texas, past metropolitan Dallas to miles of oil derricks orderly pinpricking the sky. Southward were the storied sections of Houston, Austin, and San Antonio, rich in legend from the flutterings of five flags.

So the town was a home for nearly a quarter of a million people. There were seven golf courses, five hospitals, a second rate college built around a first rate football team, and enough graft in the municipal government to admit the place to the brotherhood of American cities of medium size.

The citizens, viewed collectively, were taller than their northern neighbors, softer of speech, and slower to anger. Almost all of these citizens had a white tub and stool in their bathrooms, and those not by nature guileful enough to succeed in making a living for themselves relaxed calmly into the arms of a mothering Roosevelt government. The aesthetes got together in tight little groups, pouted and read poetry, and the unfeeling merchants took their wives to Florida or California in the winter. The water these people drank was carefully treated; they had fine medical care from birth to death, and a startlingly large number of them managed to kill themselves every year in automobiles. They lived in a world that was tightening with the threat of war, and the excitement of approaching danger, artfully pressured through to them by public print and radio, had only begun to make them stop and listen, to say aloud in their grocery stores and movie palaces that "those Japs" or "those Germans" were certainly getting out of hand.

The overlords of Fort Worth inhabited the quietest streets. Their large homes fringed the golf courses, and had three or four-car garages back of them. The interiors of these homes were lightened by pictures the owners did not understand or care to understand, and, in some cases, actually disliked. The wives of the owners were well tended and usually apprenticed to the intelligentsia. They were women who bought Shakespeare in handsomely bound volumes; they bought him and then had their maids dust him off at regular intervals. The pages were usually uncut, but the owners were proud to have captured Shakespeare so that he could not get away. They trotted about, these women, to garden festivities and quick culture clubs, and they played bridge rapaciously for high stakes.

Their husbands did nothing but make money, but they could not be blamed for that. It was all they had been taught to do, and most of them were expert in the field. They were, for the most part, patient men who had been so strongly indoctrinated with the virus of the dollar aristocracy that they could not enjoy themselves fully even when they were financially able to do so. Therefore they were principally that sad sight, paunchy American business men floundering around, flailing ineptly at a white golf ball.

And set down in the heart of the town were the children of the country-club bludgeoners, the children who were being readied to catch the torch of Business. Not all of them were like us. We were well taught, but we were taught too much, and not of the right things. We drove fast cars and we drank too much. The inference was given us, by well-bred curlings of the lip, that it was neither good nor desirable to be skilled in a trade. Instead, we were taught to prize the professions, which insisted on the profit motif in every conscious act of life. It was denied to us that there was an equal or greater dignity in building a house that would be tight against rain, or a bridge that would be stout enough to hasten the lawyers and merchants on their finite errands.

We were the inheritors in this last decade of the twentieth century. Cavin Jarvis and I were the inheritors, and the one good clean thing we had, the everlasting sense-surge, was sullied from the time we could understand the language. Sex was a greasy shibboleth. Always and forever we heard the ululations of the mock-mad censors on one side, and on the other, the one about the farmer's daughter. The little boys smirked at the little girls, and always there came a time when the girls swayed not outwardly. It was preoccupation ad infinitum. We had no great respect for our elders, and we could smell, by some strange clairvoyance of despair, the neat destruction that was being built for us.

For the time had to come when we lifted up our heads and shrugged our shoulders as parts of a troubled world. And this is the time; this is tomorrow, lately come for us. At this ripping, dream-destroying junction of responsibility and awakening, we needed a meaning as individuals. We needed it badly. The laughing boy in the White House was not enough. Religion in its present form was not enough. We had to have a real purpose, or be a part of one, and the old, carefully nurtured national legends were not enough. For lack of something to believe in, we came toward maturity as ill-met and unmannered pilgrims through a fog.

Now we are moving into tomorrow, and before too many tomorrows, we will have inherited. You may pass us on the street or shoulder us in an elevator. We will be wearing the sack suits of business and thrusting our necks rebelliously inside tight collars as we join the dollar hunt. We will be whispering hosannahs to executive vice-presidents, and we will be fretting over taxes. But our eyes will not be smiling. Too many Whitneys went down for that, too many evidences of the cheating termites in the American woodwork. Too many Senators have beamed their phoney benedictions on us, and a few too many unctuous prayers have been chanted over us. The times are bad, but the times are changing. Something has begun to move and go forward beneath the trim fit of the deacon's coat and the banker's choker collar and the old Weems' cherry tree fable. Something. . . . We are not smiling.

If we seem foolish, remember that we were young. Most of us were born with silver spoons in our mouths, and around 1935 the spoons began to tarnish. The taste of it was not pleasant on the tongue. . . .

THE INHERITORS

1

ALL the world was darkness, and I woke up slowly. I came up out of a tight prison and the light welled into the dark office and hit my eyes in painful fans. At first there was no shape or size to the world, just part of it black and part of it hurtingly bright. Those who are not cautious with bottles will know what I mean. For an unlovely honeycomb clogged my nostrils, and the musty reek of whiskey, wreathed into them. The skin on my face was stiff from the heat that had burned behind it; the joints of my body ached where the bones conjoined, and above the groin and below the ribs there was a dull battering ache, as though someone had massaged the region with a baseball bat. Iron bands girdled my head, beginning just above the eyes and gripping around to the base of the brain. I am told that this is the medulla, but it did not seem important.

The first evidence of overt action was the hardest. After I had tested the floor with my feet, I sat quite still on the edge of the cot. I was tremendously surprised with the ability of the human body to conquer obstacles, and with this thought lingering in my mind, I looked across the room. Jarvis was sitting there. Somehow I had known all along that he would be sitting there because in my mind I shall always group whiskey and spinning lights and the more acute antics of the human spirit with Cavin Jarvis.

Although it was early morning, he had on a tail coat and top hat, and his dark perfection of appearance was like the index to my thought. His sleek young head was bent forward, one hand was on his knee, and he was regarding me without any expression at all. There in the shadow he had a predatory look, short lips precise and eyebrows twisted in appraisal. Jarvis always seems to be smelling something that is not there, but you always feel like apologizing because he thinks it is.

"So you're back," he said. He did say it. It wasn't a question, and I gazed at him with rheumy eyes.

"I don't know yet," I said slowly. "Truly I don't."

He laughed at that, his lips jerking open and then closing. "Busted out again, I suppose?" He tapped the silk hat against one neatly shod foot. I shivered involuntarily, and shook my head with dignity.

"It is true," I admitted, "that I had a trifling disagreement with the Board of Curators, but it was nothing, really, that couldn't have been patched up in fifty or sixty years."

"What was it this time?" He leaned forward and drummed on the top of a chair, but I didn't answer, just kept turning my head to escape the smell of my own breath. It was hard to do. The misshapen alarm clock on the window sill kept ticking patiently, but I had nothing against it, and somewhere, outside, a chicken cawed unhappily.

"They called," Jarvis said.

"Who called?"

"Your family called."

I got up and by main force heaved myself into the bathroom and stuck my head into the yellowed tub. It was half full and I thought of staying under water long enough to drown, but concluded I was too cowardly and withdrew my head.

"What the hell did they want?"

He had followed me into the bathroom, and stood there with a bottle of beer in his hand. It seemed a plebeian gesture to me, drinking beer in a tail coat, but I had to conserve my strength. His clipped voice followed me back to the cot.

"They wanted the car most of all. Were concerned about you, of course, but the car was what they really wanted." He paused and smiled. "Seemed to think the car would run, would take them places, was functional. . . ."

He was wasting his time. It all came back to me. Something wonderful was going on inside my head. I remembered cannonading bitterly over the Jacksboro Highway, headlong after the girl in the yellow dirndl. The slender one with the bruised mouth. She was in her car and she got away clean. I never laid a hand on her, but on that turn beyond Chicken Inn I roared into a curve and flipped three times over. In midair, I had already started climbing out because my first thought was that the boys in blue would be along presently, and I had known even through the great fog that I would not be impressive in a conference. So I had traipsed down the road a way, where a Chevrolet with a slipping clutch had picked me up and brought me in to the office. Then, until now, I had slept.

"Jarvis," I said, "I have put the large pot into the small one. I have turned that automobile over so much it will not run." Which may not have been true, because I remember seeing it there at the last, on its back with the wheels spinning idly. I sat on the cot shaking my head and remembering, wishing vaguely that I had caught the girl.

"Was a girl at Massara's, Jarvis, and I felt moved to leap on her, but she fled and in pursuing, I turned the car over many, many times."

He was not upset. I went to the phone and dialed my number, thinking what nice treatment I was giving my family. Sickness held open house in the pit of my stomach, and when the familiar voice answered, I told about the situation entirely, neglecting only to mention that I had turned the car over. I plotted the whole accident, including the insane antics of the man in the brown Dodge who had crowded me into the ditch.

"There was no way out of it." And then I told them where the car was and how soon it would be out of the shop and not to worry, that the insurance would cover it. There at the last I got warmed up, and Jarvis moved closer to the phone, a flattering interest on his face. He was fanning himself with the top hat. It was not one of my best jobs, but it was pretty good. After I had hung up, I took the bottle out of his hand and drank the rest of it, my stomach jumping. He was still watching me, but I didn't mind. It was a look of appreciation.

"One more minute," he said, waving the hat, "and you wouldn't even have had a wreck." Then he called the Sheriff's Department for me, and they asked for the license number. I gave it to him and he repeated it, and after waiting with a suspended look on his face, nodded and wrote something on the wall. It seemed silly to me, that business of nodding his head so patiently when the other man was several miles away, but I didn't say anything about it. I was still too pleased by his acclaim of my explanatory ability. He told me the name of the garage and found the number in the book. They admitted they had the car.

"How much fix up?" I asked him, opening another bottle of beer.

He asked them and took the bottle out of my hand, but there was another one, although that was the extent of it.

"He says between four-five hundred dollars." Only Jarvis pronounced it dolers.

"Tell him I wouldn't consider it."

He raised the phone again, and said quietly,

"We won't consider it." Then he waited quite a time.

I figured the man was telling him what all was wrong with the car. From the way I smacked into that curve with the tires singing, I knew it must be considerable, but because I felt that I was being left out of it, I said something else. After all, it was my accident.

"Ask him where my top coat is?"

Jarvis asked him and turned to face me. "He says he gave it to your Cousin Vincent." He was beginning to smile, and a tiny roar grew in my ears.

"Tell him I ain't got any cousin named Vincent."

Jarvis' face was wreathed in utter happiness. "He says the guy that drove you away from the wreck came back and said he was your Cousin Vincent and took the coat away." He listened for a moment. "Guy says the deputies figured you were drunk. Whiskey soaked into the upholstery."

"Tell him to fix the car," I said.

Jarvis told him and was about to hang up when the roaring came back into my ears.

"Tell him he is a cork-legged liar and a thieving bastard," I shouted.

"He says you are a cork-legged liar and a thieving bastard," whispered Jarvis into the mouthpiece.

The telephone crackled wildly, the language finally becoming so bad that Cavin had to hold it at arm's length. I counted up to twelve, but the speaker was beginning to lose his fine initial fire, and I spoke to Jarvis again.

"Tell him I take it back. Tell him he is not either cork-legged."

Jarvis was oil on troubled waters; he spoke with an unguent tongue. "He says he takes it back. He says you are not either cork-legged. . . ."

The man's diction was better this time, and you could distinguish the phrases more easily, especially the ones with "g" in them. We listened in silence for a moment, and then Cavin carefully dropped the instrument into its cradle.

It was full day outside, and cars were beginning to pass on the street. Jarvis took off his formal clothes and hung them up in the closet. He had on lavender shorts, and I didn't like the note of intimacy they brought out, but I made no protest. A startling phallic fever was hammering at me. I guess the girl in the yellow dirndl was still on my mind, and I had her breasts in my hands when Jarvis came over to search for some more beer.

"That was the most toilet-mouthed man I ever listened to," he said gravely, and I nodded, wondering if the man was too mad to fix the car, but then the thought came that he couldn't wreck it any worse and that brightened me up perceptibly. But I didn't get too intellectual because I saw Jarvis' shadow when he came up behind me and began to reach around for the remaining bottle of beer. I brought my foot down on his hand, and he withdrew it.

"Jarvis," I said, "I am desolate and sick. Sick to the guts."

He was still looking at the bottle, and he was sucking his hand where I had kicked him.

"Sure," he said. "Sure. I know how it is." All the time he did not take his gaze from the bottle. "Guess we better load up on some more beer. . . ."

Automatically, I reached for my back pocket. It was, in a way, like a man drawing a gun.

2

IT TURNED into a good one before it was through. Jarvis' business was selling Mirrolites, which are illuminated house numbers. Not really illuminated, because, as he explained it to me, you can't furnish wooden markers with electric lights in them for three dollars. A loss is involved if it is done that way. What he sold were markers painted white with black numbers overlaid and reflector buttons on each side. The things lighted up before headlights, and for your money he threw in absolutely free another and smaller driveway marker with another reflecting button on it. Jarvis saw the things in Dallas, and became, overnight, the Fort Worth agency. Without portfolio, of course. His business lay with people of some substance, since the lower and middle classes cannot indulge in random purchasing. Nobody, according to Cavin, wants to know the numbers on poor people's houses anyway.

Business was phenomenal on this day. I joined the corporation on a commission basis, and went right to work. We kept on drinking beer and telephoning people, and by four o'clock we had sold nine, which was, indubitably, twenty-seven dollars in the till. Bradley took them out and installed them, and either Jarvis or I flourished up to the door and collected. Bradley was the man of all work, a bad complexioned, good hearted fellow of medium build who could drink with some distinction and sing a very husky ballad. In fact, he was much likened to Crosby until the whiskey overtook him, which point came late as a rule, and then he merely gave out lonesome croaks and often cried over popular songs, a failure for which I could not make allowance. I had known him for many years, and he was nearly as glad to see me as he was to see the case of beer.

He got back from his last job about six o'clock, and came in the door with a package under his arm. That is, he came partly in and then stopped. I was sitting with my back to him, and Cavin was lying on the couch. A small hornet had just been captured and killed by Cavin, and I was engaged in explaining the tremendous air of tragedy involved in which a hornet, meaning no offense and properly frightened, might sting a man who, in turn, had no wish to end his, the hornet's life, but had no method of expression universal enough to effect an understanding with those of the hornet world. I had, perhaps, exaggerated the incident out of all proportion to its real importance, but when I got started it was hard to stop. I was emphasizing the immense futility of it, for the hornet, and drawing a somewhat muddled analogy with respect to mankind and death. When I had finished, I spoke without looking around.

"Jarvis, I am afraid Fred has bought another quart of rose-water."

Jarvis looked at the ceiling thoughtfully. "I cannot believe," he said, "that the firm's oldest employee would do a thing like that."

Fred spoke hurriedly and in wrath. "Oh, no, Jimble," he said, "that's out. All that old stuff is out. I'm tired of doing all the work around here and then having the executive staff drink up all my wages."

Jarvis twisted on the cot. He had been facing the wall. "Bradley," he said, "you are fired. Get your money from the cashier and take your drunken, middle-class stupidity out of here. As the president of Mirrolite, I have been watching your work. You have slipped out of sight, and your number painting gets more Chinese every day. Beat it."

Fred went into the bathroom snorting. "Get my money from the cashier," he mumbled scornfully, and glasses clinked. He sat down on the lid of the toilet, and pulled the cork out of the bottle with his teeth. Just as he got it all the way out, the lid slipped off the toilet and he fell to the floor, spilling some of the whiskey. We were both regarding him.

"Bad luck," I said. "I forgot to tell you that was broken," and Cavin raised up on the cot. Fred sat there for a few minutes fuming impotently, and then, as if he did the only possible thing, he tilted the bottle and sent its contents rippling down his throat. Jarvis came up on his knees.

"You are a disgusting hog, Bradley," he said, but he was watching the bottle. Fred knew it, and when he had taken the long drink, he sat quite still for a few seconds. Then he shuddered involuntarily, but his mouth was curved upward as he arose from the floor and sat down. After he had stared at us for another minute, he got up again, set his bottle down on the table, and started back to the bathroom for the glasses. Midway he stopped, retraced his steps, and retrieved the bottle. Then, with it nestling under his arm, he went in and got the glasses.

"Jarvis," I said, "Bradley is a prime example of mediocrity. He will sit there with the finest intentions in the world, sternly protecting his whiskey, and then he will take two more drinks, and his proletarian mind won't be strong enough to refuse us a drink. As soon as that gentle warmth starts to eddy through his guts, he will crumble completely, and eventually we will have the better part of that bottle."

Bradley looked up. His broad face was filmed with sweat; he was caught in the motion of pouring another drink, and sullenness pulled at his mouth. But he didn't say anything, and we waited while he drank that drink and another one. Then another, and when that was down, Jarvis got up and walked over beside him.

"Was that it?" he asked, and when I nodded, he reached out and got the bottle. Fred started to stop him, but I cried out sharply and he subsided, a brooding look on his face.

We were almost through the bottle when Mumford put his thin face in the doorway. It was evident from his combed and brushed look that he had just dressed for the evening. Mumford was called "Hot Horse" by all of us because of an unfailing faith he had in bad horses, and there was about him the air of eternal sophomore. He wore a light blue suit and his body was meagre in it. Mumford is likened to a fox terrier by many people who are not dog lovers, and the resemblance was startling as he stood there with his head cocked to one side.

"Ah there, Jimble," he said, beaming at me, "back from the collegiate wars, hunh?"

I didn't say anything because it seemed obvious to me. After all, I was sitting there. I must have been back. Mumford was not dismayed by my silence.

"What day is this?" he barked.

Fred looked around. "Thursday," he said.

"Good!" Mumford exulted. "I am allowed to drink whiskey on Thursday."

"Good," spoke up Fred promptly. "Bring that whiskey you are allowed to drink in with you." Fred was beginning to mellow and he pronounced his words very distinctly. It was a state of slumbrous dignity he could maintain while the rest of us were vacillating. After he had spoken, he snorted suddenly, as though he were ineffably contented with himself and his construction of little humorous sayings.

Mumford backed away, determined to be angry, but the fox terrier in him was too strong. "Always kidding, that Bradley," he mumbled weakly, and came around to sit by me and beam in my eyes. I closed my eyes.

I was sitting in the darkness with the heat beginning to flow down my veins when somebody else, several people, came through the doorway. Voices called out greetings to me, but I did not recognize all of them so I played fair, kept my eyes closed, and said nothing. I heard Bill Jerry's stolen witticisms begin, and Von Perry whooped loudly. Someone else named Bumpers was introduced all around, and I nodded cordially when my name was called out. My eyes were still closed, but when Jarvis got up out of his chair suddenly I knew, even in the darkness, that they had brought a lady with them.

Cavin's manners were exquisite, and he took over the introductions with a syrupy politeness. Her name was Miss Blenheim, and when it came my turn, I bowed. I heard her pause before me, and then Jarvis said in a low voice, "He is blind."

"How bad for him!" An unsettling husk of excitement was in her tone.

She had started on when I decided to explain my blindness to her. I said that as a general rule I didn't like to discuss my mishap with others, but that she could have the story if she wished. When I had said that much, she moved back toward me and I could smell a fragrance on her. But not too much. Bill Jerry called out quickly, but I was gone by then. I began with the story of my youth, how my parents had forbidden me fireworks, and so to use them I had gotten in the habit of storing them in my navel, that I had an unusually roomy navel, and that one day I had put two skyrockets in that aperture. A tremolo was in my voice as I told of the skyrockets becoming ignited somehow, possibly by the electricity produced by my thighs rubbing together, as I had been fat when young, and that the rockets had gone off and shot me, one in each eye.

I thought I had lost her then, but amazingly, she moved in closer and put cool fingers on my eyelids. I stood very still, waiting for her to ruin it, but she said that I was a very fortunate young man not to have been hurt any worse. Her fingers were pleasant on my lids, and I got one of her hands and kissed it. It was a stupid thing, but I did it and opened my eyes. It was the girl in the yellow dirndl, the one who piled up my family's car on the long curve. Of course she didn't have on the yellow dress. It was a flaring blue skirt now, and tight pink sweater which she should never have worn except in a closet, and then only if alone. She was smiling and her eyes were long-lashed and crinkled at the edges. Drinking had flushed her oval face, and her mouth was slick with paint. She came only to my shoulder, and her black hair fell in long whorls.

"You are a very blue-eyed blind man," she said.

"And you are a very deceitful Lorelei," I answered, and we stood there looking at each other and then I was smiling too. It seemed as natural as breathing, and we continued at it with people drinking and talking around us and skeins of hazy blue smoke drifting up through the light. Bill Jerry got worried after awhile. He could not understand how two people could possibly be smiling at each other without lust or profit unless they had a reason duly executed into law and reposing in archives. That, I suppose, is the reason he got worried. Anyway, he took her off, and I walked over to hear just why Jarvis wouldn't consider movie stardom.

3

THE party was at its peak when Wilfred arrived. He came through the door swiftly, a shuffling, bareheaded fellow of thirtyish age. The stoop in his shoulders and the elegance of the apricot velvet jacket he wore gave him an alert and insouciant air. Until he spoke, the air of buffoonery lay deep, but his piping voice brought it out like a naked thing. He came swinging into our crowd of gentle intoxicants and began a business-like circuit of the room, stopping for a word with everyone. He gave me a moist, peremptory handshake, as though I had not been gone for seven months, and then went on. He was possessed of the tremendous dignity of the very drunk and his phraseology was a queer mixture of Gainsville County jargon and the patois of kings and queens. When he had spoken to everyone he knew, he sidled over to me again and spoke in a raucous whisper that echoed out over the valley.

"The major portion of these gravebent and ill-fed residents I am known to," he said, "but who is the girl in pink?" I did the honors, Wilfred beaming at my side.

"Miss Blenheim, Mr. Wilfred Garvey, Cattle Speculator."

Miss Blenheim looked at him. The drinks she had taken lighted that high excitement in her eyes. It was unsettling, Wilfred fawned long over her hand, and then, suddenly, left us standing there. She stared up at me in silent question, but I motioned to her and we watched him proceed. Buddy Perry was sitting on the cot with a slatternly looking girl that Fred had produced by some alchemy of flat rocks and recent rains. Jarvis had already proclaimed the girl to be as common as hog tracks, but she sat there with a drink clutched in one hand and she was smiling through dirty teeth. Wilfred went up before her and pointed like a bird dog; he stood transfixed, gazing at the ghoul with a steady eye. It may have been that he was moved by some nostalgic memory of plowed fields in Gainsville County, but he did not move until Buddy arose and performed the introductions. The square faced girl shook her Dutch bob and smiled at him. We couldn't catch all of the conversation, but it was animated and in the course of it, he left off all pretense and just stood there with his hands on her hips, patting those ample curves and testing them with playful slaps. All the time he was looking straight down into her face, but suddenly he turned and stalked back across the room toward us. He was halfway when a thought struck him, turned him around.

"Perry," he called out in a high clear voice, "I think you can get some of that."

Perry began to protest that he already had a wife, but Wilfred was indifferent. Having passed judgment, he put his head down and went to the desk for a drink. Bradley was standing there shaking with rage.

"Not that, Garvey," he shouted angrily, "nothing like that. . ." The girl was his date.

But Wilfred was involved with Jarvis by then. Jarvis had berated him for not bringing any whiskey and was discoursing in a flat voice on Wilfred's antecedents and his eventual end. Wilfred glowered at him petulantly, his purple silk ascot askew.

"You ain't got nothing, Jarvis," he said. "Used to be your family could light a shuck with any of them, but no more. You got a puss on you like a decayed angel and you live in a house with statues in it, but you ain't got nothing. You are through. You are deader than Kelsey's gonads."

Cavin regarded him thoughtfully. "A dirty little sharecropper in circus clothes," he murmured. "Might know this would happen, might figure some of you clods would think this was a free country. We let you come in and take a drink with your betters and this is the thanks we get for it." Cavin was overcome with the venom of his thought; he rocked back and forth on small, neatly shod feet. "You addlepated fool from the country," he mused, "it is known to us that the ape caught up with your mother."

Miss Blenheim caught hold of my hand and I wondered where Jerry was. She was standing on her tiptoes and I saw that she wore no stockings on her tanned legs.

"Is it always like this?" she asked, brightness over her face.

"Not always," I said. 'They get more profane sometimes. They are all of them looking for something . . ."

She took the handkerchief I held out and wrapped it around her hand. It was that hot. Then we held hands again.

"Maybe they are looking for that most ephemeral bluebird," she said, looking up with her lower lip caught in her teeth.

"And in your Christmas Pie, madam!" cried Mumford joyfully. He was going by with two drinks.

"I guess they don't know themselves," I answered, and then the girl with the wonderful teeth came over. She was crying because of the way Cavin was talking and she wanted me to stop it. About that time Wilfred took a long swing at Cavin. It was nothing more than a Sunday punch aimed at the world, and he nearly dislocated a shoulder. Jarvis, by some legerdemain, came out of the corner swinging a hammer, and he slowly forced Garvey across the room. Wilfred's arms were up in defense and his weathered face was working. The hammer went swishing through the air in long arcs, and it was close. When Wilfred was backed into the far corner, he began to writhe and shrink like a dervish of fear, and just as I was beginning to wonder whether or not murder was on the program, a slow husky voice started up in the room beyond. We had all fallen silent to watch the attack on Wilfred, and we turned toward the connecting door.

"Dusky maiden . . . dark and sullen . . ." It was Bradley. He walked to the door and opened it, stood there leaning back against the jamb. He was jolting us with the song, and there was, unmistakably, a jungle fever in the room, an upsetting excitement. Fred had us; we were drunk and helpless. Softly, across the room, Jarvis began to pat the broad surface of the desk; Mumford rapped out a deeper note on the panels of the door, and I upended a chair and began to spank its bottom lightly. The girl next to me was humming and the others took it up after her, a rising murmur under the infectious torrent Bradley was pouring out as he stood braced in the door. He had on a cork sun helmet and Boy Scout shorts. He looked ridiculous but he didn't sound that way and we picked up the tempo until it was a solid savage booming that smashed into the ears. It came to be a strident and overwhelming lament, and Wilfred came out of his corner and lifted up his cracked voice. We pounded our makeshift drums until our hands were past feeling, and the girl in the pink sweater started swirling in the center of the room, undulating to the terrible insistence of the sound that we were making in the little room. Her thighs were white blurs as they scissored under the ballooning skirt, and the wench with the Dutch bob came out to join her in an abandoned trucking exhibition. The whole room seemed to sway.

"Jungle sweetheart . . . dark and sullen . . ." Fred had stopped singing and was shouting, bellowing out an atavistic wail. All of us, banked around the whirling girls, were swinging back and forth, rapt and queer smiling. Wilfred's jaw was slack and his eyes burned. He lunged suddenly and reached out but he got the wrong one.

I stepped back into the bathroom and picked up a pitcher of water. Then I stepped back again and threw the contents into Fred's face. He coughed and ducked with a strangled sound, and the core was out of the madness. Jarvis trickled off on his desk beats and Mumford gave a few last tentative slaps on the bottom door panels. He had knocked the others out. For a moment, there was hushed silence. They all began remembering. Slowly they pulled away from their Congo fires, and Hot Horse Mumford took a drink, his thin hands shaking. Jarvis stood where he had been, smiling faintly, and Wilfred drew one hand across his mouth.

"Jesus!" he said. And then, "Jesus Christ Almighty . . . !"

The girl in the pink sweater came over and sat down by me on the cot. She asked why I had thrown the water on Bradley, so I told her.

"Garvey is impulsive. He just grabbed the wrong one, Miss Blenheim."

Her eyes were steady on me. "What was the difference?"

I spread my hands in polite deprecation. "There is no comparison. So there can be no talk of difference." Then I got us two drinks. She put hers down thoughtfully, at one shot, and I decided there wasn't anything about her I didn't like. As I watched, her forehead creased.

"What do you think of me?"

"Miss Blenheim," I said, "it's not time for that."

She was annoyed. "My name is Lucille," she announced, "and I am engaged to be married."

The thought was irrational and unexpected. I wished she hadn't told me because then there were three of us sitting on the cot, but I didn't protest overlong because some policemen came in and we all went to jail.

The city was, at this time, building a new city hall, and we were taken to the old post-office building. There we learned that our wailings had broken the peace and that we owed a debt to society. After an interrogation by a bulletheaded desk sergeant, we handed over our valuables and followed the turnkey down a dark hall, where we were locked up in a crypt.

The whole thing was executed with dispatch, even to my offering to have the badge off the sergeant before morning. It was when I said this that he wrote "drunk and disorderly" after the other charges. He was a patient man, and I suspect that many who passed that way coveted him his badge. When we were in the cell, Mumford started to laugh, but in the very heart of his mirth, coughing overtook him and he began to heave. His thin shoulders shook and he reached into an inner pocket for his asthma remedy.

It was in a small tin box. He pulled the box out, still shaking, and poured a little mound of the grey powder onto the lid. Then he fumbled out a match and lighted the powder. It burned with an acrid smell and he bent over. The two other prisoners in the cell with us looked on with great interest.

"Breathe deeply," I instructed him. "You are not long for this world, so breathe very deeply."

He did. He leaned forward and inhaled the twisting thread of smoke like a man making a strange obeisance. He hunched forward and sucked the stuff into his lungs. His hands were cupping the tiny glowing spot centred in the grey powder.

"It is a hell of a thing," said Bradley dejectedly, "when five . . . six men have got to take a cure for something only one of them's got. That damned stuff is choking me to death. I don't believe I know Mumford this well."

The Hot Horse grinned, all slick teeth in a narrow face, and his fingers folded more closely around the smouldering medicine. It was not really very interesting because I had seen Mumford before, and just as I was dropping down into sleep. I heard Garvey cry out that if he was not released his children would have no lunch money at school. It was too flimsy, and the turnkey grunted in derision and went away.

When I awoke it was still dark, and Jarvis was standing out in the corridor. Why he was not inside with us, I could not say. How does the music get into a violin? I asked him where Lucille was.

He put his hands on the bars. "Lucille who?"

I cursed him then, because he was aware of my taste in such matters, and he told me that the girls had been released. I pondered the knowledge.

"Well, why haven't we been released?" I asked, but he only shook his dark head, as though releasing us was out of the question. Then he took a pocket comb and began to work on his hair. The gesture annoyed me beyond reason, and I sidled over toward him.

"Remember when you kicked me on the hand?" he asked, picking stray hair from the comb and smiling faintly. I said that I remembered and was sorry, and then I reached out and got him by the lapels. I nearly drew him through the bars. Mumford struggled up and sat watching me manhandle him. Wilfred was snoring rhythmically in the far corner.

"Jarvis," I said, and tugged him lovingly, "Jarvis, let's get the ball rolling . . ."

4

WE WERE released shortly before noon. Our lawyers had come down, very sleepy, before daybreak, but their efforts were of no avail, principally because of the tone I had taken with the desk sergeant. Finally we stumbled out into the sunlight and stood there blinking. Jarvis was in a cafe across the street, and he came over to meet us, a crisp gentleman in fresh linens. I called up the Biltmore Garage and had my Uncle Harry's car sent over, and then I drove Bradley, Garvey, and Mumford home. The great silence had fallen on the Hot Horse; he was snuffling audibly and his face was drawn with worry. Fred was whistling and Wilfred was still half asleep. When they had been dropped, Jarvis suggested swimming and we drove out to the club.

The long clubhouse hugged the curve of a green hill. Shrubs and trailing ivy softened its sides with shadow, and the faded roof soaked in the sunshine. Midday somnolence had glazed the swimming pool's surface until it was a green mirror, save when some bird curvetted down and flecked its smoothness with thirsty stabs. The bases of the tall trees were locked in shade, and a faint clatter came out of the club's kitchen. Unseen tennis players spatted a ball behind the high shrubbery around the courts, and sprinklers whirred up slow crystal fans down the fairways. Two men in knickers were bent almost double on the sleek putting greens, and as we walked along under the cool portico, Cavin and I could see stout Mr. Busby flailing at his drive from the first tee. A morose caddy was slumped over an enormous bag, and the blackamoor was watching patiently. Mr. Busby sliced his ball in what was nearly a half circle, and as it was passing out of bounds the little man threw back his head and sent out a bitter rush of words. He was caught there before us with his bald head thrown up, cursing under yellow sunlight, and as we watched, the black caddy stooped and took another ball from the pouch on the bag. Then we turned out from under the porch and started toward the pool.

The lifeguard was sprawled in his orange deck chair. He was a lean man with a mahogany body, and even the hairs on his chest were burned a golden brown. Dark glasses gave him a fiendish look as he dozed in the full sunlight.

His right foot was propped on its heel at the end of the canvas chair, and there was a soft crinkled look about his toes, a pleating of flesh about them that the water had made. His mouth was ajar, as though some high dream was marching in his mind. Perhaps he was not altogether unaware of his predecessor, who had flexed his muscles to great advantage two years before when Mrs. Werber, a dark and excitable widow, had taken him off to be her very own in holy wedlock. Perhaps Seth, the present guardian of the pool, had given himself over, in sleep, to a life like that, complete with tweeds and shooting sticks and golf and yearly travel. It was the most probable explanation of his beatific smile as he lay with one arm outflung.

When we had rounded the corner of the pool we stopped, and Jarvis passed his hand tentatively before Seth's eyes, but the sleeper moved not and we looked at each other thoughtfully. Then Cavin turned and walked into the locker room. When he came back, a long piece of twine was in his hand. He dangled it before me but I shook my head.

"I don't follow."

A sneer tugged at his lips. He bent down, looped one end of the string around the big toe of Seth's doubled leg and gathered the slack. The other end he made into a slipknot and dropped the small noose around the guard's right ear.

"Not so!" I said, backing off. "It will pull the ear right off his head."

Jarvis was looking down at his handiwork. He smiled. "What the hell," he sniffed, "they got him insured."

I tried again. "The string's too damned strong . . ." But even as I said it, Jarvis bent to tickle the upraised foot, and without further protest I faded into the shrubbery. The brown man twitched a few times, and the toes on his roped foot twisted. Jarvis was squatting down, well to one side, and he kept up the tickling. A car passed through the hot asphalt beyond the hedges with a slight sucking sound. Cavin's brow wrinkled in impatience as he worked on the foot, and a few locks of his dark hair fell down across his face.

It was cool back in the shrubbery, and just as I was settling down, Seth's leg shot out and the string tightened sharply. Then was the stillness usurped, and a wail of fierce anguish went up as the brown man flopped out of the striped deck chair and clapped both hands over his ear. He threshed around on the grass, biting his lips in agony, and two negro chefs came out of the club house to hear his wild alarums. They looked toward the pool, shielding their eyes from the sun, but they could not see the prostrate figure because of the stone balustrade that encircled the wading pool, and after a moment their white caps went bobbing back into the bowels of the kitchen.

The first harsh lamentations had dwindled to a low ululation of sorrow by this time, and the grieved Seth began to examine the string. He was so recently come from pleasant sleep that it took a long time for the sabotage element to penetrate, but when it did, he ripped off his dark glasses and stared around wildly. One hand was still clutching the injured member, and blood was dripping from his fingers. I looked for Jarvis, but he was not in sight. I didn't look for him very hard because I didn't want to make a lot of noise and attract Seth, who was methodically searching the premises. He went through the bathhouse, ducked in the towel room, and even climbed up on the diving towers. Finally he gave up and started down the sidewalk toward the clubhouse. He was still clutching his ear, and the ruddy drops of blood were still pouring out from between his fingers.

After I had gotten the car, I drove out of the gates and stopped, and soon Cavin came up from in back of me somewhere and got in.

"He was right mad about it," I said, "and I was correct about it tearing his ear."

Jarvis wiped his forehead with a white silk handkerchief. "No reason for it to ever get this hot," he said. "Guess we better go hunting tonight." Then he lighted a cigarette. The flare of the match was pure yellow.

"Same place?" I asked, and when he nodded, I agreed it was hot. "Be a good afternoon to go swimming, though," I concluded.

Cavin turned his head slowly and looked at me. A thin film of sweat slicked his perfect features.

"Jesus," he snapped irritably, "you saw him jump, didn't you? You can't have everything." He lolled back against the seat and sucked deeply on the cigarette. "It cut him," he said happily, "like a knife. . . ."

5

THAT evening we went back to the club for dinner. Over a hundred people were sitting on the lawn, grouped around long tables bearing bright napery, dull silver, and shining glassware. The people made a very pleasant tableau as they chattered and gestured. They were all well dressed and aware of it, all grouped in families or clotted together by business ties, and they represented an absorbing and purposeful arrangement to those who knew them. The grass beneath their summer shoes was closely cut, and the darker green of the hedges and shrubbery banks was painstakingly manicured and rimmed by precisely planted flower beds.

A stranger visiting the scene, diners sitting in late afternoon sunlight with whitecoated waiters bustling about, would have thought the place Utopia, for the ingredients were surely there. Everyone present was important in one way or another, and the long weathered clubhouse was like a benevolent frame for them. Good food they had, ease, and drinks frosting in cool glasses, together with beauty of a sort in the tailored lines of the white swimming pool, its emerald surface barely ruffled by the breeze. But Cavin and I had been there before, and the tended faces bent over the good food were all aligned to memory.

Because I had been gone, I sat and studied the people sitting around us. To some I nodded and smiled pleasantly in those vague genuflections people go through. As my eyes winnowed through the whole bunch of them, the thought came that all the faces had certain associations. This one was weak, that one strong, rich, lascivious, or clever, and each one went into the mind through the eyes as more than a single person, but rather as an index to a family and an attitude and a way of living.

After we had ordered our dinner, Cavin took a bottle of Scotch from his pocket and poured both of us a drink. When he did, a lady in a gargantuan summer hat snickered in disapproval and whispered to her husband behind a gloved hand.

Cavin nodded to her politely, downed his drink, and sat savoring the fumes from the empty glass in exaggerated happiness.

"Ah," he said to me, "it is straight-life Alfred and his charming wife." Then he continued the elaborate business of sniffing his empty glass and I munched my salad.

Alfred Jeffers was a rotund insurance man. He had a head like an early tulip, and he was always more gracious than any man has a right to be. Life is not that good, but considering the fact that he was betting against death, perhaps it was nearly that good on the cropped grass where he sat and smiled so earnestly. The pimple crop on his round face made him look like a diseased cherub. He was a man greatly given to extravagance in speech.

His mother had been a very good, although not inspired, seamstress in the town, and Al gave his beginnings the direct lie on every occasion. He had been quite successful in enticing the local gentry into buying policies, and he lived in a burnt brick mansion with a sagging roof. The sag, artfully engineered by an outlander architect, was costly but impressive, and people whose houses had straight roofs were properly respectful. His place was filled with furniture of all periods, and the total effect, to the discerning eye, was the history of interior decorating wrapped up in one house.

Jeffers' hair was so thin as to allow a dull sheen under the remaining strands, but he could, with some difficulty, order a meal from a French menu, and the ability charmed him beyond belief. He was a very successful man and he and his austere wife ruminated through their dinner with a satisfied air.

But they were not people you could watch for very long. After a few quick glances, ennui set in. The sun was slipping down behind the trees along the road, and in its fading light were scarlet stripes, flung through the trees. A caddy cried "out a' bounds" faintly for some late players trudging up the eighteenth fairway, and as we watched, one of the distant figures dropped another ball and flailed away at it.

I had another drink with Cavin and lighted a cigarette. The whiskey pooled its warmth in my stomach and exploded gently. It was an old and remembered pleasure, and we had another to tamp the feeling down. Then I leaned back in my chair and watched Jarvis. He was posturing, struck still in a pose for a collar advertisement, and his chiselled features were clean. I was moved to speech.

"Jarvis," I asked, "how much do you like yourself?"

He grunted and kept his pose. I could not deny that it was decorative, the black hair curling down to his collar and the young profile hung against all inspection like a newly minted coin. When he turned and blurred the image, I knew somebody important had come in.

It was Broderick Warstler, and a horde of people were following him across the darkening lawn. Warstler came toward the tables with an easy swinging gait, as though he knew nobody could stop him.

He was a tall man with a bronzed face, and there were scars beneath his eyes, small livid scars that separated him from the assembled company. In passage, he threw remarks back over his shoulder, and when he did the people trailing him would laugh loudly.

Waiters materialized without warning from under the club veranda, and a whole pack of them was standing at his table when he came to it. A very blond girl in a black linen dress was immediately behind him, and she took the seat to his right. The rest of the company arranged themselves around the table. They had all been drinking.

Warstler was a symbol of the offchance encounter with fortune. He was a barber from Abilene who had found oil. Without oil, he was as nothing, but with millions attendant on the discovery of an oil pool, he became something to titillate shop girls and astonish models.

Many tales were told of his meteoric rise, and they were all startling, like the man himself. Some said that the Federal Government had given him ninety days to show cause why he should not be indicted for oil fraud, and that in the allotted time he had skidded a rig, drilled an oil well with two wrenches, a rusty wireline and a prayer, and had opened the north Burnett field with only two days of grace.

So shadowy is the line of conduct among men, however, that in one gush of the earth's black blood, Warstler suffered an incredibly swift change from potential felon to actual millionaire and acceptable figure. Wealth cushioned his background in the burghers' eyes, and they sent their daughters past him in fine raiment. As yet he had made no choice, and seemed a trifle contemptuous of their cultivated stolidity even while he danced and moved about with them.

The curious scar patches under his eyes had come from his days in the fields. They were the places where a swiftly moving line had wickered and gobbled at his face. He wore an enormous ruby on the middle finger of his right hand, and the glinting stone was noticeable when he gestured to the people at the table. The ring was, in a way, a symbol of the man and the suitable, lucky Shangri La he had reached.

Jarvis stared over thoughtfully. "All that dough is burning the hell out of him," he remarked.

"He doesn't look so upset to me," I said, and chewed my steak with great relish. "He looks like he's having all the fun. Wish I had me a pig like that one in the black outfit. Anyway, he's one hell of a lot better than those ones." I gestured with my fork and the lady sitting across from us arched her brows.

The man I had stabbed at with my fork was Bryan Fogerty, and he was having dinner with his wife. He was a compact man with thick glasses cutting across his wide face, and a high choker collar pinched at the loose wattles of skin on his neck. A set expression was always sealing his lips, and I couldn't remember ever having seen him smile. He was beyond fifty and his wife was somewhat younger, a lanternjawed woman with bugged eyes and braids of wisping grey hair. A mulish preoccupation pursed her lips as she and the equally serious Bryan concentrated on the feeding process.

They made a silent spot among the more loquacious diners on the lawn, and the way they spoke and moved, everything they did, was part of an unconscious protective coloration. Fogerty was the patriarch and moving spirit of the club; he had been one of the charter members and he still roamed about the grounds, stepping cautiously in his high topped shoes and peering with slumbrous dignity into every cranny of the place.

His wife's father had been one of the real Western cattle barons, a lusty Yankee conquistador blessed with a blistering tongue and an uncommon eye for cattle. He had moved into Texas in a lurching prairie schooner, had been no whit tougher than his time demanded, and legend had it that his fortune had come from standing on the rutted trails leading into Fort Worth and buying culls and "down cattle" out of the great herds moving overland.

Stubbornness and shrewdness, plus an ability to remain alive, had brought him an empire on the staked pains, and he had lived in a great gingerbread mansion dressed in bastard cornices, cupolas, and turrets. In his last hour he is reported to have produced a bottle of whiskey from under his mattress, and when the priest arrived to shrive him he had said simply, "get that bastard out of here . . ." Then, after another stout suck on the bottle, he had resolutely turned his face to the wall and died of having lived, an angry old man with violent memories locked up in his head, memories of spurs and silver conchas and tossing seas of longhorn heads moving through trail dust.

And so his angular daughter, the daughter of Sudden Tom Barlow, had married a pompous little clerk tending to fleshy jowls over a choker collar. Old Tom must have spun in his grave at her extreme reversion to Methodism, but under Bryan Fogerty's manicured hands, the fortune waxed greater than ever. In fact it became so great that it took all of his time and all of his wife's time to care for it. They had few other pleasures, and even now, as they sat at dinner, the two of them seemed to be brooding over judicious methods of financial preservation and increase. They were very careful people and ate every bite of their salads.

Jarvis turned from them and looked at me. He was licking his lips. "Can't be happy . . . ," he mused. "Too rich. Been rich too long, and they aren't people any more. Just deadheading along until they get cold."

I had still another drink, although not a large one. "What about Warstler there?"

"Different. Entirely different. He's just passing through his money like a thirsty man passing through a green country. He's using it, making it buy him things. He knows there ain't no pockets in a shroud."

"It could be," I answered, and crushed out my cigarette. "Maybe they ought to lock the people up in the bank vaults and let the money do the living . . ."

He looked up, startled. "Maybe you ought to have another drink and think that one over. I don't think it's ready for release yet."

There was some truth in what he said. Heat was beginning to rim my face and burn behind my eyes. A few lights blossomed on the second floor of the clubhouse, and their advent put friendly orange blurs in the dark windows. My eyes were still ferreting through the crowd, and they came to rest on George Sorrels. I didn't call him to Cavin's attention. I just sat there with the whiskey warming me, watching and pitying him.

George was entertaining a party of eight. He looked haggard as he presided over the gathering, but his wife, Laura, was shunting the conversation about with practiced ease. Her exquisitely waved hair and bland smile were the very epitome of interest as she wheeled from one guest to another, and she laughed with almost insane merriment at every sally. I was watching her go through her paces as mistress of the dinner revels when Jarvis tapped me on the arm.

"Get a load," he said, sniffing, "of her eyes."

I looked, not seeing at first, and then it came to me. Above that carmined and constantly smiling mouth, her eyes, when viewed steadfastly, were absolutely dead and unblinking. I nodded to Jarvis, and we watched her in silence.

Sorrels was a lawyer. He was not a forensic flame before juries, and he was no genius in the more difficult matter of preparing cases for trial. Indeed, he was something considerably less, but he had the vague air of authority that comes to successful barristers, those surgeons of people's affairs who operate with scalpels of paper writs and subpoenas. His name was old and honorable in the community, and one member of his clan had been a Supreme Court Justice of Texas. His face was square and had an urban look, a smooth tired look. He played golf in the eighties when alone, and in the nineties when with clients, and he had been a good halfback at Yale. I had not known him then, since I had not been born, but I understand that he was a minor sensation in the Eli backfield, a squat blond Texan wont to rove through enemy territory.

He was graduated neither too high nor too low, bought his way out of the World War, and returned to his native heath, where, after a few years, he had married a cunning visitor from Virginia. This visitor was the vivacious Laura Penfield. On this night, George was not marked by extreme vitality as he sat entertaining his friends, and the long years must have taught him that being blocked in and smashed by an enemy tackle was merest child's play. Because Laura was a bitch.

The jealously guarded culture of the Virginia Penfields was a symbol rampant in every gesture she made and every word she said. Without giving the matter any particular thought and, indeed, without pressing, she had managed for many years to spend at least twice what George made over any given period of time, and the Sorrels' progress from one big house to another was accompanied by a lavish of parties for the local great and near-great.

The many movings were caused by rental troubles, and even on this night George's name was posted on the club bulletin board for a three-figured item. So perhaps George might be forgiven for a slightly dyspeptic expression as he sat with his knobby friends around a table on the greensward, and it may even be that his wife's high laughter came to him as slightly monotonous mood music in the weary business of life.

I handed my glass over to Cavin. "Think you'll ever be a big man like George?"

"Not if the Lord loves me at all," he said, intent on pouring the drinks. There was not a great deal left in the bottle, and I was grieved to see a marked discrepancy in the size of the drinks.

I received and was drinking the stunted portion of the remaining whiskey when I saw that Jarvis was pointing like a hunting dog. When I turned, I saw that he had lighted the windows of his soul for the benefit of a lady sitting at a small table some distance from us. She was smiling enigmatically, and because of her strange costume, she looked as though she might have come with the lowering of the dark. She was not alone, and as she gazed languidly across at us, her companion shrugged back and began to talk over his shoulder to an obsequious waiter.

At thirty-eight, Frank Harkness was a local legend with stomach trouble. His golf was expert, his manners flawless, and he wore clothes that were excellently cut but never obviously new. It was said that Harkness' valet broke in his master's shoes before that gentleman ever put them on his feet, something like the aging of wine or the business of putting mileage on a sports roadster.

He was a slender man, stooped and brown, with tiny red veins clouding his eyes, and one of his shoulders was higher than the other. His family had gotten a great deal of money together in real estate, and for awhile Frank had played good, careful polo, in which sport his saddles were lined with silky white fur and quite amazing to us, his neighbors. But the polo interim in his life was short and it was probably the nearest to a violent thing he ever did, because when it was over he toiled not, neither did he spin, save when a few too many drinks had wetted his flaxen mustache and given him pause.

We knew everything and nothing about him, which is to say that we knew his family, the size of his house, the number of his schools, and the physical appearance he made. He went to New York when winter came, and in the summer returned to his stone mansion overlooking the fourteenth tee. Not in the memory of the club's oldest servants had he been ruffled or angry, and he gambled well, drank many drinks, and spoke with the somewhat strange eastern abruptness, although not in a loud voice. Down through the years we had heard many stirring tales about him, some in the locker rooms and some filtering through from other parts of the country, as of the time when he had ridden a motorcycle up the broad stairs of the club and around the narrow gable on the roof. He had been drunk, and when he fell, the servants had rushed to the spot where he lay under the smoking vehicle in time to hear him say, quietly, "Ask Bert to tell Mr. Jory that I will not be able to play this afternoon." And then he had fainted away under pressure of the pain from his broken legs. Stories had been told, too, of his boudoir besiegements and they were probably all true.

In the beginning these things had been wonderful, and the recounting of the time he had thrown the visiting Countess into the swimming pool when she was insufficiently clothed was pure adventure, but as we grew older we came to feel that he was a hollow man. Then such things as his epic speech from underneath the wrecked motorcycle became only evidences of his rigid conduct mechanisms. When we first began to realize this, his whole air of aloofness became understandable. He was the symbol of a propriety that had defeated itself, and he said very little because he had so little to say. He was tired now, and he drank more than ever.

The shadow of nearly forty years grew deeper in his eyes; they became more thickly veined and impenetrable. They had a baffled, swimming look in them. He still awed us a trifle, because even after he became only a well dressed nonentity with plenty of money and stomach ulcers, we were moved by the absolute consistency of his conduct, the deliberate way in which he wandered through life half asleep, half drunk, and immured from anything dangerous, making not the slightest imprint on his time.

The exotic lady with him was Marsha Manning Locker, and she was being regal beyond belief. Some women have children and some put up preserves, but Marsha Locker cultivated the regal air. And she had been doing it long before the shadow barons in Hollywood found out how to spell glamour.

She had the willowy figure, the dead white skin, and the huge eyes necessary to the role. It was all a studied effect with Marsha, and she dramatized herself constantly. On this evening she wore a rich purple burnoose that wreathed down around her throat, and her slender arms were moving constantly, gloved hands twitching again and again to Harkness' sleeve. Lipstick that was almost black made her mouth a bruised blotch, and her teeth were too white between the slashing part of her lips. Shadow hung like blots beneath her staring eyes, and her eyebrows were absurdly thin and fluted.

She played the Lady of Darkness very well, but then again, it was all she did. Lacking freshness of a virginal sort, she worked the languor angle up to the very teeth, which in her case were false, but exquisitely so. Rumor had it that she was a drug fiend and that she was constitutionally opposed to wearing undergarments. The first charge we suspected but could not verify, and the second was provable on any windy day. Perhaps she believed in preparedness.

Her hands were her most striking features. Even as Cavin and I watched, they kept fluttering constantly from hair to lip to table, and the only time they were completely stilled was when they were out of sight. She played golf in gloves, ate in gloves, and never accepted invitations to play bridge because there one must deal and shuffle the cards, and there were no nails at all on her fingers.

I had seen the restless hands quieted once, when she had fainted at a dance, and her fingers were beautiful, long and tapering to smooth ends but without any vestige of cuticle or nail. She had been concealing those unusual fingers for so long that even when she wore gloves she kept up that odd and entirely graceful fluttering. It was an art form, and Cavin and I watched it appreciatively.

Cavin seemed to be going through a mental strip tease and I knew why. Unkindly, I said, "I wonder if it's true that Charley sold her to

Nate for fifty thousand dollars. . . ."

Charley Manning had been her first husband, a rotund broker who had gone down in '29 with the rest of America, but shortly thereafter had come bursting back into affluence after a Mexican divorce. Even while speculation was highest, Marsha had walked among us tranquilly, offering no explanation, and shortly after her divorce she had married Nathan Locker, a tall Jew with greying hair and many mercantile millions. To her, the change was no great inconvenience as she had only a few hundred yards to move. It was not like Charley had picked somebody all the way across the golf course.

Locker died in three years, and she proceeded to take on a dynasty of the young men around the club. One at a time, of course, and with great discretion. None of them lasted over six months, but as they passed by, numbers were attached to them by the watching citizenry and scathing comments flew as to their daily virility, so that finally the business of patting the satin with Marsha came to be a real distinction. Those who had stood their period at stud were listened to with some deference.

However, she was at the moment pivotal between Jarvis and a young lawyer named Jorgens. This vacillating frame of mind strengthened our conviction that Marsha was growing old, but on the twilight lawn, she seemed ageless and Jarvis continued to regard her with great intensity. It was a part of his campaign.

I ordered two Scotch-and-sodas, and then prodded Cavin again. "Does it feel like fifty thousand dollars worth to you?" I asked.

He was rapt. "How would I know?" he whispered.

"All right," I said. "How would you know? That statement makes you either a vegetarian or a coward. And where were you last night, this morning rather, at four o'clock?"

Our waiter brought the drinks, and Cavin took half of his at one gulp. "I was waiting for a bus."

"Those big buses must have a hell of a time getting all the way upstairs in Marsha's house," I said, and he grinned slightly.

"It's no matter," he said.

I snorted. "Of course not. But it is good, isn't it?"

"I don't remember." He was still smiling faintly down into his glass. "It's really none of your damned business."

"Not while druggists still sell salvarsan, it isn't," I answered, and lifted my drink.

He made no answer, and I glanced around at the others present on the lawn, but it was growing darker. Nothing had changed much; I could see enough to realize that. As we sat there, the waiter whisked our plates away and replaced them with smaller ones bearing conical mounds of pale green sherbert. Up on the porch of the clubhouse, unseen musicians struck up a lively discord of violins and saxophones, and their earnest efforts floated out over the heads of the diners. Apropos of nothing, I said, "what's the good in it?" and Jarvis stared over at me. His eyes were smooth, glazed by drinking, and they did not blink.

"I know," he said sulkily. "The same song and the same singers. We're not people; we're just a set of attitudes walking around with logic-locked approaches to everything in life, and thirty phrases locked up in back of our teeth . . ." He stopped and sneered.

I took no offense because he was despising everyone there, and I could not bring myself to resent it. A black hand hanging out of a stiff white sleeve was about to spirit my salad away, but I cautioned the hand and it withdrew. Jarvis was still staring at me, but I started to work on the salad, which was gay with artichokes and bannered with pimento.

"Thirty phrases," he said again, and tweaked his nose angrily. The strings of the orchestra rippled again on the porch, and the white jacketed waiters kept scurrying about among the tables.

"These ones are all clean and neat as pins," I put in, and then foolishly suggested that we leave while we could still walk away.

"Thirty lousy ways to express all we think or feel," he insisted. "Jesus!"

"It is certainly a shame."

He lifted his head at that, and refixed the obsidian stare.

"You don't have to stay," I went on. "Exits have been provided that will allow disgruntled patrons to go away at will. You could get two yards of black calico and be another Messiah. You could live under a bridge and dilate your nostrils lovingly at little children. You could give out any number of pamphlets."

He hadn't moved, but when his jaw tightened I knew he was angry. He got up from the table and started across the lawn, stepping swiftly on his small feet, and I went with him, murmuring over his shoulder. He was going very fast and he was bowing to people as we passed. His pace made the bowing look a trifle silly. I closed the gap.

"If the whiskey ever drains out of your face," I whispered, "it will crack open like ten-cent china."

He got to the edge of the lawn and turned around, swinging his head from side to side. The music was a rustling murmur and the twilight was swirling around the gay tables behind us. He made no comment, only looked at me as I shook his unyielding hand.

"Jarvis," I said warmly, "I am glad to be back. I have admired you for a long time . . ."

We were standing there when Fred drove up.

6

BRADLEY was wearing a battered Borsalino hat, and I guess he had been drinking too, because he drove out to the city limits on the wrong side of the parkway. Cars scattered before us like quail; we could see their lights dip as they drew up and stopped or turned across onto the grassy plot separating the sides of the boulevard. I was sitting in the middle and on the close ones I would tense up just the least bit. Whenever I did that, Jarvis would sniff and wrinkle his nose. We went along that way, like a prow through parting waves of traffic, and Fred kept humming softly and tapping his booted feet on the pedals. One car came thundering toward us, and I had the unpleasant thought that it might be somebody we knew, like Hot Horse Mumford, but at the last minute the other driver swerved and went bouncing across the middle of the parkway. The sound of his horn dwindled behind us, and Bradley threw back his head and laughed.

"Where is it?" I asked.

"Back of you." Bradley grunted it.

Our tires screamed faintly going into the junction road, and I rummaged around the top of the seat until I found the bottle. I didn't shop around, just unscrewed the top and let it pour. It was bad and I felt the tissues of my throat rebelling. Cavin tilted the bottle and tried it.

"God!" he said, spitting the amber fluid out of the window, "God Almighty, Fred!"

Fred was humming "Sweet Leilani." He shrugged and sang softly that nobody had forced us to drink it. "You asked where it was," he chanted, "and it's not like . . . tum-te-tum . . . you paid for it . . ." His bumpy face was entirely satisfied where the dash light touched it. He got a lot of satisfaction out of the fact that he could drink whiskey that gagged both of us. The old Buick went catapulting down the road and the town receded behind us.

When we got to the dump, Fred pulled off the main road, and we bounced down a rutted trail to our usual parking space. I hadn't been there in a year, but there didn't seem to be any change, only that the garbage was piled higher. When Fred switched off the lights and cut the ignition, the motor gurgled into silence and we sat there for a minute listening to the dolorous croakings of the frogs.

Far across the conical mounds, we could see cars passing on the highway, and as Fred fumbled for the bottle, we could hear the staccato rhythm of the night flyer bound for Denton. We couldn't see it because the shadowed humps were in the way, but we sat there and listened until it was only a faint thunder fading into silence.

"Like to be aboard," said Bradley. He was leaning forward over the steering wheel, his head cocked.

"Why?" Cavin put one leg out of the window and lighted a cigarette.

"Don't know. Just movin'. Goin' somewhere."

Cavin inhaled deeply and smoke fanned out of his nose. "You keep on driving this bastard like you did on the way out here," he said, "and you'll get someplace. Quick, too." He spat out a speck of tobacco and released that sniff of his. "This place stinks like ten thousand whorehouses."

There was a rotting fragrance in the air. It was a stench that arose from the heaps of waste piled in front of us, a stench born of decay. We got out and loaded our guns in front of the headlights. Bradley was using a twelve-gauge, and Cavin glanced over at it.

"You're a hell of a sportsman," he said. "Thought I told you not to use a shotgun any more?" His anger was real; his dark eyes were alive with it. Bradley shrugged and went on shoving shells into the chamber of his gun.

"Sure," he said, "sure, you told me, but as yet you ain't bought me another gun."

Jarvis snorted but made no reply, and we walked over to the knoll. We were carrying our seats, and when we got there we placed them three feet apart and sat down. Fred and I were using camp chairs, and Jarvis had a shooting stick, one of the kind that you spread the handles on. The ground was soft and the chairs bogged down some, but once you got them firmly set they stayed that way. A slight mist was rising, and Fred went striding through it to place the hunks of cheese. I had the lamp resting on the arm of my chair, and Cavin and I sat there waiting for Fred to come back. He was cursing softly and I flashed the light on his feet. He had stepped into something, and rotten orange pulps were clinging to his boots. He sat down beside us, still muttering, and we waited for the rats to gather.

Ten minutes passed. The moon drifted under the clouds, and we could hear a faint scurrying. Cavin whispered something to me, but I didn't move.

"Let them get bunched up," I called over in a low tone. "Remember how they used to scatter?"

Cavin didn't answer me, but his voice was sulky as he cautioned Bradley about letting both of us get in shots before he turned loose with the heavier gun. Then we waited another minute, with the scratchings getting louder.

Cavin's gun spoke first. I had to switch the light on; its strong beam leaped out and fixed the churning grey rats in an oval of light. Cavin had a snap shot into the group and one of the sleek bodies quivered and jumped just before I fired. I couldn't tell anything about mine, and then Fred's gun blooped and the whole white circle seemed to be filled with jumping rats. When I switched the lamp off there was a great silence, for the frogs in the marsh beyond had been quieted by the sound of our guns.

"Not bad," I said. "Got a whole slew of them."

Jarvis clicked his breech sharply. His voice was angry still. "That murderous sonovabitch of a cannon that Fred's using takes all the sport out of it."

Fred got up without saying anything and walked into the darkness. We saw his flashlight pencil around, and then he came walking back.

"Got seven," he announced brusquely, and I put the beam around to where he was standing. Seven torn rats were dangling from his gloved hands. They were big ones, nearly a foot long, and the blood from their wounds glistened black under the light and dripped onto the ground. Their teeth were yellow and their eyes, set in narrow heads, were beady.

"That one," said Jarvis, pointing with his cigarette, "will go near three pounds." He whistled softly.

Fred was angry. He threw the big rodents away and we heard their bodies patter to the ground. Then he said he was going to the car for a drink. He stood before us, a brooding statue, and then he suddenly turned and walked away.

Jarvis and I sat there smoking and waiting. The moon came out again and under it you could see the dark forms begin to slink across the rubbish piles. It was hard to do, but when your eyes got accustomed to the gloom you could see them moving through patches of moonlight. It was a funny thing, but they always got thicker after we had killed a few. I suppose the blood of the dead ones must have caused that, because after some of it had been shed, they seeped out and went toward the bait like short shadows with glinting eyes. We had three more shots at them, but Bradley didn't come back and we let them rest.

Cavin was a good shot, better than I was. Often he would call out his target by position in the group, and then that particular rat would kick. "Top one on left," he would whisper, and his gun would go off. We were about sixty yards away and it wasn't bad shooting, in that light. The second time we turned loose, there must have been fifty rats caught in the spotlight. They were a roiling mass, and all you could do was fire into their center. Both of us emptied our magazines, but when the live ones had scuttled away, there were only five or six dead left. It was hard to see how we could have missed that many times, but Cavin said it just proved how many the shotgun had been getting. The next two times we had a chance for individual shooting, and I got one that was just slinking out of the light. It made me feel good, to catch him before he disappeared into the darkness. After that, we waited some more. The smell of the place hadn't bothered us after the first few minutes, and I was thinking about going after a drink when Jarvis spoke.

"You glad to be back?"

"Not particularly," I answered, and waited. I knew he didn't give a damn about whether or not I liked being back, so I waited.

"Not many changes. Same people, same stuff . . ."

"Yeah?"

"Yeah." He said it and sniffed. "You are much too intellectual for that Blenheim girl. Better if I take her over; make a show horse out of her. What the hell, you got yours . . ."

A breeze stirred around us.

"I told you once," I said, "and I'll tell you again. She is mine, every juicy pound of her, and you'll get tagged for your trouble."

He straightened up and spoke sharply. "You'll drop her too hard," he said. "You always do. You are a dirty bastard."

I didn't say anything and he sucked deeply on his cigarette. The tip of it flamed. He twisted irritably, then slumped down and began to talk. His gun was slanting from one arm and he made a silhouette like a drowsing sentry. His voice was flat and matter-of-fact. He said that I had been a fool to come back, that I was a fool anyway, and that we were all spurring the hell out of things. He said that we weren't quite as funny as we thought we were, and that he didn't even trust himself anymore, that there was a line that marked the difference between drunken hell-raising and something else, something that scared him. The rats went pattering across the dark junk heap as he spoke, and the breeze stirred again and washed over us.

He was still talking when Bradley came up and stood behind us. The talk stopped abruptly, then, and Cavin began to reload his gun. The frogs were beginning to croak again.

"One more round," I said, "and we'll get out of here."

Nobody moved, and I reached for the lantern. I asked Fred if he was sitting in but he still didn't say anything and I flipped the light switch. He moved then, all right. Over my head, his shotgun sounded with a burst. He triggered it until it was empty, and then he stood there breathing heavily. Neither Cavin or I had gotten in a shot.

His fire had laced into the assembled rats like knife blades. They whirled before us as though they were being flung about at random, and after he was through shooting, they were a bloodied pile of nothing recognizable. Only one long grandfather seemed to be whole, but just before the light went off, he started to crawl away and we could see that his hindquarters had been shot off, so that his progress was a clawing antic done with the front feet. When the light winked out, Jarvis arose and folded up his seat. He didn't say anything and we went walking back toward the car. Bradley was still breathing heavily.

After we had stowed our stuff away, we stood around the car. Fred took a drink he didn't need and offered one to me. The Scotch I had drunk at the club was just a memory, and I did need one, so I took it. When I was through, Fred handed the bottle toward Jarvis but he refused it curtly. I lighted a cigarette and gulped at the smoke, drew it deep into my lungs. When it was out, hurting my nose, I spoke to the night air.

"If it's a deadly matter," I said, "you both got guns, and we might as well get a great big rat killed before we go home."

Jarvis shifted and one hand went up to button his coat. Fred didn't say anything.

". . . but if it's not a killing matter," I went on evenly, "you are both acting like fools."

They were standing close together, and when they didn't move or acknowledge my attempts to create a peace, I got angry. I didn't reach but a little bit and my gun went off over their heads. Not very far over their heads, either, and I emptied it. About the third shot, Jarvis flopped down and Fred went careening around the back of the car. The silence rolled in again as I blew down the smoking barrel.

"You crazy sonovabitch!" rasped Cavin, from the ground. "Oh, you stupid no-good sonovabitch!"

He got up and Fred came back around the car.

"Fun's fun," Bradley said, "but Jesus, Jimble, them was mighty close." It was the most complaint I had ever heard him make.

"Never saw anything like it," fumed Jarvis, brushing off his clothes. "Here, Fred, give me a drink of that whiskey."

He took a long drink and we got in the car and started back toward the main highway. They were both still upset, and Cavin claimed I had nicked his hat with one of the shots. The brim of it was sliced a little, but it looked like an old mark to me. They had quite a field day and even brought in my parents and environment. Bradley was speaking to me, very earnestly, about the folly of it as we turned onto the highway. He nearly banked into a truck while he was berating me.

"Truly, fellows," I said softly, "truly, I am sorry. You must both forgive me."

That brought on a new and more caustic outburst. It seemed that I was going to get smart about it, on top of everything else. I sat there in the middle with the whiskey heating me, and I even offered to buy another bottle of whiskey when we got back to Ballinger Street Drug Store. Bradley stomped down viciously on the accelerator when I said that. As the lights of the town grew before us, I wondered idly whether or not I had really hit Cavin's hat. I was thinking about it, smiling at the thought and glad to be home, as we rolled down the road with singing tires.

7

WE HAD headaches the next day. It was a rainy day, too bad for tennis or golf, so we were doing business. Jarvis and I were sitting in the Mirrolite office and Bradley was back in the paint shop. We could hear him humming faintly. Like true executives, Jarvis and I had our feet on the battered desk as we plotted our sales campaign for the day.

"Got the Ridgelea list?" Jarvis asked. I handed him the list and he smoothed it out. Ridgelea was one of the town's most exclusive residential districts.

"Pick out the oil men," I said. "First the oil men and then the bankers. The oil men got all the dough, but they haven't had it long. They'll think a Mirrolite is just the thing."

He stared at me absently. "Muscle the parvenu a little, hunh?"

"Yeah. Where did you ever hear of the parvenu?"

He grimaced, the handsome face wrinkling. "You forget," he said, "that I was in the Black Horse Troop at Culver."

"That's true," I said. "I forgot. Forgive me."

"Really nothing," he answered graciously. "Forget it."

He started dialing a number, and I got up and walked back toward the paint shop, thinking about the formality that was always between Jarvis and I. It was a wariness, almost, like a constant dipping of color guards.

Bradley was hunched down in one corner of the shop; he was a stocky spectre holding a paint gun, aiming it at two rows of Mirrolite panels. A thin fog of white paint was all over the room, and the smell of it was sharp. I retreated to a window and sat down on the sill.

Fred's face was absorbed; it was a square visage pocked by acne or drinking or something, I know not what. He was wearing the faded Boy Scout shorts, and a handkerchief was wrapped around his head. From where I was sitting, I could see the ridging muscles in his bare thighs, just above the knees, and the tiny drops of white paint that had been blown upon the hairs of his legs. He was a painstaking worker and often retraced a panel if it looked scantily covered. All the time he kept up a snorting noise.

When he switched off the spray-gun, I threw the window all the way up. He turned at the sound, and smiled at me.

"Really puts it out, for a little gun," he said, and started unwrapping the big handkerchief from around his head. I murmured that the gun certainly did do a good job, for a little one, and then I praised his work. It was presumption, because I hadn't ever seen another paint gun in my life and hence could not tell how a bigger one would work, but Fred took the praise so well, so happily, that I could not help being authoritative. His ravaged face beamed as I talked, and he was still smiling happily after he had dismantled the gun and begun to scrub his head and forearms with a turpentined rag.

"Jarvis doin' a little sellin'?" he asked.

"Yes." I was pointing out the spots he missed with the rag. "What is all that snorting and bellowing for, while you're painting?"

He looked up; he was serious. "Keeps the paint out of my lungs," he said. "Big danger in using one of them things is getting paint in the lungs. I'm trying to avoid it."

"Thing to do," I said. It didn't seem logical to me, because he had to inhale once in awhile, but, anyway, my mind wasn't on the paint in Fred's lungs. I wanted a drink. The rain whispering outside the windows was getting on my nerves. I was thinking of that magic drink, the one that is down about the middle of every bottle, when I realized Fred was still talking to me.

". . . don't understand how he does it," he was saying, "and it's the damndest salesmanship I ever heard of, but he sells the things. Been doing it ever since you left for school. Insults people and then sells them!" Bradley's thick mouth twisted petulantly, as though Jarvis had destroyed the set pattern of good salesmanship. "I just can't understand it," he said.

"It is fairly new," I admitted, and then we started through the toilet into the other side of the office, Bradley still pawing at his cheek with the odorant rag.

Jarvis was rolling a cigarette between his thin lips. His sandaled feet were still on the desk, and the jacket he wore sagged away from his tanned chest. He would roll the cigarette all the way across his mouth, then bring it back, and in the middle of the return trip, he would clutch it between his even teeth and take a drag. It was interesting to watch. His right elbow was propped on a chair-back, and the hand above it held the telephone.

"Give me one good reason you don't want a Mirrolite," he barked into the mouthpiece, and Fred looked at me and motioned irritably with the rag. I sat down on the casting couch and waited.

"All right, madam," said Jarvis in a cool voice. "Now don't get excited about it. There's no legislation says you got to buy one. Don't get horsey about it."

He listened shortly, after that, and started rolling the cigarette back across his mouth. Fred whimpered with real anguish.

"Tell you what you do," Jarvis went on, after the pause, "you just take one of those bell-mouthed kids of yours and ram a flashlight down his neck. Then put him out on the curb. Serve the same purpose as a Mirrolite and give the little dullard something to do . . ."

He turned to us. "Lovely children! She says she's got lovely children, old lady Henderson does. Ain't that a scream?" He sniffed and spoke into the phone again. "Madame, I've got a police dog, but I wouldn't let my police dog . . ." His voice trailed off and he shook the telephone and said hello two or three times.

"Guess she hung up," I hazarded from the couch, and he nodded. Mumford came in the door shaking raindrops from his hat. He was pointing his toes and grinning. Bradley nodded to him, and Jarvis' glance flicked up once and dropped. Mumford bowed, thin arms akimbo, pointed his toes and began to glide around the room.

"Oh rattle up a June bug, a butterfly, a bee," he sang, "Oh the girls won't let my tallywhacker be. . ."

Bradley started laughing and the Hot Horse nearly killed himself on a few more turns and flourishes. Cavin was watching him through narrowed lids.

"How does that go?" he asked suddenly. Mumford stopped dancing and repeated the words to him. Jarvis looked over at me, but I didn't say anything. That made him sore, having to ask.

"Sounds pretty good," he said. "Tricky?"

"Sure," chimed in Fred. "Sounds swell."

"It's all right," I said, and Cavin began to tap his feet lightly. A chicken outside the window emitted a sad cawing sound, and Mumford revolved again, flexing his arms. Bradley was watching and he began to hum in his husky voice.

"All right!" said Jarvis suddenly. "What's keeping us? Let's get some production on it."

Fred nodded and Mumford peeled off his damp coat. Cavin went out of the room and came back with a new roll of toilet paper. He put it in my hands, and then went out again, with the others following him. I was still thinking about how good a drink would feel, how neighborly to my stomach, and I didn't try very hard the first time, just muttered something about the June Bug Boys in the third aria from the Tallywhacker opera. I made the announcement, but nothing happened, and Jarvis came back into the room.

"Stinks," he said. "You're not trying. This is a class act, dammit, so give me some production on it."

He tied a piece of string on the light fixture and knotted the roll of toilet paper on the bottom end. The roll hung down in front of my face.

"What I need is a drink," I said. "I just haven't got it, today."

Jarvis was hurrying back to the other room. He mumbled something over his shoulder about getting a drink later, and I leaned forward toward the bulky roll.

"Station X.E.R.," I intoned, "Dr. Krinkley's station in quaint, greasy Mexico. Next we will hear Dr. Krinkley's theme song, 'Isn't Love A Gland Thing?' . . ."

Then I waved my arm and turned around, and the three of them came swinging sideways into the room. Their arms were linked and they had a choppy glide step. They were pretty good. They rattled up the June bug and the butterfly and the bee, and then when the girls wouldn't let their tallywhackers be, they got a nice daisy-clipping rhythm with Fred's deeper boom holding up the two light voices. They went across the room, swung around in unison, and strutted back the way they had come. They stalked into the bathroom looking across at me with cocked heads. I started laughing and Mumford put his head back through the doorway.

"The girls won't let . . ." he hummed, and then, as the toilet flushed with a liquid roar, "my tallywhacker be!" and the other two heads popped out suddenly and joined him in one last barbershop chord.

I was clapping loudly when Jarvis walked back into the room. He looked very pleased.

"It was all right, wasn't it?" he asked, and when I nodded, he sat down at the desk and began to tap on his teeth with a pencil. "Yeah, it's all right. We'll have to work up a whole routine."

He was as highly pleased as I ever saw him when somebody was not in actual pain. I batted the dangling roll of toilet paper with one fist.

"No," I said, "we won't work up any routine. We got lots of little pleasing stuff like that, but it would be too much trouble to work up a routine. We won't do it."

"It was pretty good," he said, nodding his dark head and tapping with the pencil. "It was all right."

The other two came back in the room. They were both breathing hard, and Mumford's hands shook as he lighted a cigarette. While we listened, Cavin called four more numbers. Two of the people weren't at home, one of the others bought, and the last one hung up with a sharp click when Jarvis wondered, aloud, whether or not she had three dollars. The rain had stopped and a pale gleam got through the clouds. We could hear the chickens begin to circulate under the window.

"Into every life a little rain must fall," I said, and Mumford looked blank. Bradley's head came up.

"It's early yet," said Cavin mildly. "Not dark yet. Won't last 'til midnight if we start now." He was mild about it because he wanted a drink as much as I did. Mumford had a vision, and gave his hands a dry washing.

"Get liquored up, hunh?"

Jarvis picked up the phone and called Ballinger Street Drug Store. After he had placed the order, I discovered that I didn't want a drink anymore. But that was no new thing, and I knew I would want one by the time it got there. Bradley wagged his head.

"Seems as if we put every nickel of our profits in hard drink," he said.

"Kind of a sinking fund," I suggested, just to keep my hand in, and Hot Horse Mumford was dervished with laughter, more laughter than I had expected. It was gratifying. Even Jarvis was smiling, and we sat there and waited.

Buddy Perry beat the delivery boy in the door by about thirty seconds. It was an amazing knack he had, that business of showing up just in advance of the whiskey. He knuckled his blonde thatch and grinned widely when I removed the paper from the bottle, and he insisted that we have a short prayer before we partook of the contents. He said that it was a blessing his family had used at the dinner table, before the depression, and he chanted it gravely, speaking of the blessings we were about to receive and asking divine guidance for the future. Mumford stood through the ceremony with a slightly horrified expression, and his eyes were fixed on Perry's hands. The hands were folded lovingly around the neck of the bottle. Jarvis sat through it without smiling, and only Bradley bowed his head. Whiskey was that important to him.

Midway through the bottle, I told Perry my little joke about the sinking fund and he received it well, so I decided to add it to my material. It was nearly dark outside, and we sat there drinking and laughing until the bottle ran out. Then we counted our resources, and finally found a $5 windfall in Perry's watch pocket. When he got up from the floor, where we had placed him for the search, he was minded to be angry, but a few slugs out of the second bottle convinced him that we were right after all. The haze rolled into the little room, and another hour found the talk more random and profane.

"Let's go down to the Wayside," suggested Mumford, "and trap some beavers."

"Won't do," said Fred, smiling hugely from under his sun helmet. He nearly always wore the sun helmet after it got dark. "Mumford," he announced, "you ain't got nothing. You are all washed up as a lover."

"Fact," shouted Perry, flailing the table. "Goddamned fact, and you realize it full well, Hot Horse."

"What you think." Mumford leaned back in his chair, and Jarvis stuck one foot out and tipped the chair over.

"I don't know," said Cavin, as Mumford hit the floor, "he might catch a syphilitic club-foot and do some good."

Mumford got up and poured himself a drink. His shirt was torn at the elbow, and his pants were dirty. Bradley was shining his shoes on the edge of the couch, and he shook his head sadly. Von Perry whinnied.

"What about if he had a wife?" he asked. "What about that?"

"Yes." Jarvis considered the matter. "I'll bet he could get some if he had a wife."

"Sure he could," I said, "if he got her drunk enough."

Mumford's face altered from amazement to anger. He was greatly vexed, and he started to give Perry the metal edge about other marital situations. I thought it best to change the subject before Perry erupted, so I broke in and told them about the Laughing Room. I felt good. The unrest was gone out of me entirely, and there was a faint fire down my veins.

My voice was low in the darkening room. Lights were blossoming down in the valley as I talked, fuzzy skeins of light that shifted before the sight. From time to time, somebody would reach out and whiskey would go into a glass with a gurgling sound. Fred was leaning forward in his seat, and Mumford was standing behind him, very thin in the semi-darkness. Perry was propped against the wall, over by the bathroom door, and Cavin was a silhouette by the desk.

I told them all about the room, the Laughing Room in the White House. There was a stir and a halfhearted chuckle from Perry as I advised them, solemnly, that the President was entirely nuts, that he had this room where he went, late at night, to cackle over the shape he had gotten the country in. I explained that, of course, government officials couldn't allow such news to get out when the world was so troubled. Jarvis sniffed audibly as I showed them how news of a depraved American president might lead to disastrous foreign action. Mumford caught his breath when I told of the newspaper correspondent who had fallen asleep in the White House one afternoon, and had been awakened at midnight by that maniacal laughter. My voice tightened and fluted up a full octave as I described the President, pealing out the names of his various alphabetical projects and howling with glee.

"Just like that," I concluded, "just gets in there, in that room, and goes eyaheyaheyaheyah!!!"

I threw back my head and released a flood of brazen laughter, and Bradley flinched in his chair. Then I stopped laughing suddenly, and took a drink, the only one moving in the room. Finally Perry's chair scraped and he got up.

"Well, hell," he said. "I guess I better be gettin' home." There was a sheepish smile on his face. "You got the goddamndest imagination, Jimble," he said, "of anybody I ever knew."

He went out the door, and after a minute, Mumford put his hat and coat on. "Don't think it ain't been charming," he piped. "Guess I'll get a ride with Von." He went out and we heard his light footsteps retreating down the driveway. Bradley got up, took a drink, and stalked into the bathroom. Cavin turned his head to look at me.

"Not bad," he said. "You nearly ruined it, once there, with that correspondent crap, but it was all right."

He took a drink and I could barely see the cords in his neck tighten. When the drink was down, he offered me a cigarette and I offered him a light. His face was blurred to my sight; it had a shifting quality, as though it were out of proportion. As I blew the match out, the toilet flushed loudly.

"Ah," Jarvis murmured, "a lark!"

I didn't say anything, and in a minute Bradley came back in and had another drink. He was standing over us, his head up as he drank, and I asked him what time it was. He put the glass down with a click.

"Now?" he asked.

We had a longer silence then. My stomach growled faintly, and as I recalled the speed with which we had dispatched the whiskey, I couldn't blame it.

"No," I said gently. "No, Fred. Not now. Tell me what time it is in a little while."

He was content to let it stay that way. He nodded and sat down on the casting couch, and Cavin shook his head slowly, as if in despair.

"Tonto Club dance next week," he said, to no one in particular.

We could hear the passage of cars on the street out in front of the office. The cars made slick sounds as they went by on the wet pavements, and as I sat there Lucille began to dance in my head. I could see her white thighs moving under the ballooning skirt, and that startling fever began to burn inside me.

"We be pretty drunk after awhile," whispered Bradley from the couch, and since there was no denying it, I stretched out and made myself as comfortable as a man can who doesn't know what time it is.

8

WE RESTED the next day. With the Tonto Club dance only a week away, Jarvis said we would be foolish to dissipate our vitality so we lay under the hot sun all morning. Of course, there was the troublesome matter of our dance assessments, but they didn't have to be paid until the day of the affair.

The Tonto Club was a group of young men in Fort Worth society who had banded together for social purposes. The membership was composed of gentlemen between twenty and forty, bachelors all, but you didn't need a whole lot of background to become a member. If you had a good job, a pleasant speaking voice, and the appropriate raven dress, you were admitted on the theory that you could help pay the way of other members with better families but less money. It was a very democratic organization, and every year it gave two dances, one in the summer and one at Christmas. The dances were most festive, and brought out the best in our younger set, so it was almost imperative that one make an appearance. We were sitting out on the lawn in front of the office talking about the possibilities for frolic when the phone rang inside. Jarvis leaped up and answered it. I lay back down, shielding my eyes with one hand.

It was long distance, Rick Walton calling from Austin, where he was going to the University. Jarvis talked to him, only he did more listening than talking, toying with a pencil and sniffing lightly, as though he smelled something unpleasant. He said "fine" a few times, "yes" twice, and then he said "okay" and hung up.

"Rick Walton," he called out the window. I made an appropriate noise. He went on to say that Rick was flying up that afternoon with a friend who lived in Dallas, and that a party was to be given that night, since classwork would call him back to Austin the next day. I sat up and blinked at Cavin. He was a vague shadow back of the window.

"Sounds all right to me," I said. Rick's uncle owned, among other things, the largest hotel in town. It was a fact which unavoidably tinged our thought toward him.

"He says it's got to be a closed proposition, just the three of us. Said Bradley was out. Said he sang too damned loud."

I shrugged and scratched my bare shoulders. "What about dates?"

"He says get him a date with Dorothy Barney."

"All right," I said, heaving up, "get him a date with Dorothy Barney."

Jarvis picked up the phone and dialed a number. He lapsed shortly into his negro dialect while talking to the maid, and then took on a gentler tone while he spoke to Dorothy. He fixed it, and when he was through, I walked in out of the sunlight and took the phone from his hand. I had a number in mind, and sure enough, Lucille answered.

"I thought maybe you'd be in jail," I said, and she hung up. I tried it again. "Joke," I explained. "They can't all be good."

She softened. "They don't have to be that bad."

"I am so sorry. Where is that fiance of yours?"

She said he was in Houston, and I said that I was overjoyed and would she give me a date? I wanted the date badly, and I could feel my pulses pounding as she hesitated.

"Very sedate, very," I promised, and crossed myself with my free hand.

She finally answered. She said "Yes," as abruptly as though she were mad at herself. I couldn't resist the temptation.

"If you wear that sweater," I said, "you had better bring me a pair of boxing gloves."

"You go straight to hell!"

She hung up again, but I was amused beyond all reason. I was thinking about it, wondering at the strange feeling of anticipation I had, when the Hot Horse walked into the office. Behind him was Buddy Perry, unsuccessfully trying to dance along in the loop of a lariat he was spinning. Mumford draped his skinny form over the drawing table and began to read the paper. Perry threw the loop at my head. I ducked it easily, and he began to cast at the doorknob. After many tries, he finally roped it.

"How's that?" he asked us generally, but no one said anything and he began to coil the rope. He had a square quart bottle of gin hidden inside his jacket, and he brought it forth, together with a carton of ice and four lemons. He looked considerably less bulky when all the stuff was on the table, and after he had laboriously bisected the lemons, I made a drink.

Mumford looked up from the paper and gave a short whistle. Then he began reading an article in the paper. It was all about the effects of the depression, with several paragraphs concerned with "disenfranchised" youth. Mumford read that last part with considerable feeling, and then stood there shaking his head.

Perry yawned heavily. "We the lost generation, hunh?"

"Sure," I said. "We're one of them."

"Oh." He licked his orange tooth and reflected. "What we lost from?"

I grinned and gulped at my drink. "If we knew that," I said, "we wouldn't be lost."

Mumford started cracking his knuckles and walking around the room. His long legs scissored swiftly. He looked like a fledgling stork in a loose suit, and he clutched his narrow brow.

"Doomed characters, that's us," he said, staggering over against the wall, "bein' battered around by a ugly world."

Perry was watching him. "It's shameful," he said seriously, and took a quick nip out of the gin bottle. "How came us to get in this terrible shape?"

Cavin laughed suddenly, a cackling burst of laughter. Mirth shook his shoulders for a minute, and then they stilled, but a last trace of amusement was curling his lips as he looked over at Perry. He shook his head unbelievingly.

"I would never have thought," he said, "that a human body could exist for twenty years without any brain directing it."

"Don't speak to me," said Perry gravely, "for I am a very tragic character."

Mumford wandered back over to the casting couch and fell on it. Dust motes spurted up and danced like specks of gold in the sunlight from the window. Cavin went on plucking the hairs from his nose, wincing when they came out. I walked over to mix another drink and found that the lemons were all gone but I squeezed the rinds carefully and got a sufficiency.

"Tell me about it, Jimble," said Perry suddenly.

I crossed the room with my drink and sat down. "Tell you about what, Von?"

He dropped down out of his chair and came across the floor on his knees. His hands were fluttering with idiot rapidity around his unshaven chin. Mumford raised up on one elbow, and Cavin turned his dark head.

"Tell me about the place," Perry whined, "tha' little place we gunna have . . ." He laughed craftily, and sneaked a look around at the other two.

"Oh that," I said. "You never get tired of hearing about that, do you Von?"

"Naw." He waggled his head violently. "An' the fatta the land. Tell about the fatta the land, too."

"All right," I said. Cavin was shaking his head again, and Mumford's gaze was intent. "We going to have this little place," I said in a musing tone, "about a half-million acres, just enough land so we won't have to say boo to nobody for help, and we'll have a few oil wells on it, just a few little gushers, and we'll have a couple of good friends down in Austin so we can run all the hot oil we want to . . . We'll have a shiny Duesenberg to ride around in, and we'll eat off solid gold plates and we won't wear nothing but old Harris tweeds to work in, and we'll have such good lawyers we won't have to pay hardly no taxes at all, and we'll just sit around sipping Canadian Club and being happy."

"That's it," babbled Perry. "That's all guys like us want, ain't it, Jimble?"

"That's all guys like us want," I droned on, "just a little steam furnace to keep away the cold, and a little house with six master bedrooms . . ."

"In case," said Perry warningly, "that's just in case . . ."

"In case somebody came by and wanted to stay the week with us, or if they wanted to stay longer, why they could, and couldn't nobody stop them."

"An' the foxes," broke in Perry, dancing on his kneecaps, "you left out about the foxes."

"And we'd have a whole slew of black foxes and you could take care of them, Von," I said, patting him on the upturned face with one hand. "You could go out every day and worry them, and by and by their furs would turn grey from worry, and then they would be very valuable because they would be silver foxes and we could sell them for a pot-walloping price. And then we could get some more black ones for you to worry. We'd eat simple stuff like artichokes and pheasants and we'd just stay there on our little place and be happy."

Perry whinnied and shivered with rapture. "And I could clip the bonds, too, couldn't I?" When I nodded, he grinned happily and sighed. "That's all guys like us want," he said.

Mumford whistled incredulously, and Cavin looked up at the ceiling thoughtfully. I took another pull from my glass, and felt the heat loosen me. Perry got up and dusted off his pants, and then he walked over to pour a drink. The colorless liquid arched out of the square bottle and mounted in his glass. The chickens were clucking contentedly outside.

"God Almighty," said Cavin softly, "I hate myself for being weak, but sometimes I just don't know."

He raised the tweezers toward his nose again, but a smile came instead, and spread like contagion until we were all whooping. The chickens stopped clucking at the sound of our mirth, and Perry stood by the table with the drink in his hand. He was blinking, and every once in awhile he would give a jerky bow.

"It's no lie," he said earnestly. "That's all guys like us want."

When their gin was gone, Perry and the Hot Horse tried to borrow two dollars, and, after failing dismally, left the office for an unannounced destination. Cavin and I were flipping cards at a felt hat when Bradley came into the office. His face was grim, he needed a shave, and a cigarette was dangling from his wide mouth.

"The last time," he said, "it's the last time."

Then he started shrugging out of his overalls. When they were off, he clumped over to the closet and threw his heavy sack in it. Jarvis was slumped against the wall fingering the deck of cards.

"Bradley," he said, "what you cannot see is that our first consideration must be the honoring of contracts. If people call in and order our product, there then exists an implied contract between them and us, which we are in all honesty compelled to fill."

Fred straightened up, staring at him. "Yes," he shouted in a trembling voice, "but this crap of making me go out and steal back the ones we've already installed so we can fill new orders is pretty damned sorry."

Jarvis was deprecating. He ran his thumb over the cards. "We have more reflectors ordered, Fred. You know that. You know they have not come. It is a case of sheer necessity."

Bradley went back into the paint shop growling, and I got the deck of cards from Cavin and started flipping them at the hat again. They twisted and fluttered irritatingly, but I didn't mind. I was thinking about Lucille. When I walked over to pick up the cards, Jarvis was laughing silently. I looked past him and down over the valley, a green hollow in an earth that was beginning to darken. The airliner from Amarillo came cleaving through the flung splendor of the sun's last light and passed on to the north. Bradley's paint gun hissed behind me, and cars went charging by on the street outside.

"Jarvis," I said slowly, "we are going to get drunk tonight and I sure dread it."

He stirred and I heard a match scrape on the wall. "I know," he answered. "You always hate it." He paused for reflection and sucked deeply on the cigarette. "But then again, you always get drunk . . ."

He went on talking, but the rest of it wasn't important. I stood before the window with my stomach quivering at the thought of getting drunk and my mind vaguely troubled by being forced to be alive in the same world with Adolf Hitler. The duality of these unpleasant streams of thought was jarring. As much as my egocentric nature would allow me, I tried to feel compassion for all the little people that Herr Hitler would finally throw into a trough of thunder.

I tried to convince myself that I should not get drunk at the hotel, that I should be at home ruining my eyes over ponderous tomes concerning the Really Important Things in Life. I tried to think of one thing I could have learned in four colleges that would be an index to avoid fear of getting drunk or fear of being killed in a war started outside my ken and not touching me in any way.

I tried to think of all my elders had taught me, and I tried to believe that some things were worth dying for, worth being gallant for, or even worth thinking of before sleep. But all my thoughts were flawed; they were all false rabbits and the hounds of belief would not run for them.

All I could pin down was that I was almost a quarter of a century old, that I did live in the best country (for all its shortcomings) in the present world. Beyond that I only knew that the total of all men had written in books and limned away for endless time in grave considered words led directly away from my time and my particular spot in infinity.

All the splendor, all the precious things that I had locked up in my head so carefully, salvaged out of childhood, all that was only a few handfuls of confetti littering up the eternal picnic grounds when the revelers had passed by. Standing in the half darkness, searching for something to believe in, I sensed this and I said that it was all right, that I didn't care.

But I did care.

9

WE PROCEEDED with utmost decorum toward the party for Rick Walton. We dressed carefully, put correctly colored ties around our necks, hitched up our socks with fancy garters, and donned summery, double breasted suits. These were the suits that our fathers wore; they were the suits shown in the windows of the stores, and they confronted us constantly in advertisements. Even over the radio, unctious voices praised their sturdiness and beauty, not to mention quality of fabric and distinction of line. I suppose they were good suits. Everybody wore them.

But not everybody wore them like Jarvis did. He was trimly proportioned and carried himself well. On this night he came out of the house in a white jacket and deep blue slacks, with a pale blue tie set in the forks of his shirt. When he got in the car, I said that everybody would be wearing the ensemble around the country club before long. He sniffed and lifted his lip in a precise sneer.

"That's your tail," he said, fingering his freshly shaven chin. "I had these especially designed for me on the coast. I'll be damned if any of the peasants around here can get them."

I did not doubt that he would be damned, eventually, but I knew he was lying and he knew I knew it, so we did not press the point.

When we had picked the girls up, we made very small talk on the way to town.

There were five of us altogether, Jarvis, myself, our dates, and Dorothy Barney. They were all nice girls, but, excepting Lucille, not inclined to be intellectual balls of fire. Rick's date, especially, tended to be confused by almost anything, but, as Jarvis said, it was an adventure to watch her walk. As he put it, "both halves of her buttocks whispered lovingly as they passed, and when she took a full step, they turned a corner, like monkeys fighting in a sack."

Lucille was trim in black, semi-ruffled, and Cavin's date, a Miss Foley, looked as though she had been heated to a liquid state and poured into her dress, which was red velvet. The only untoward incident occurred when Cavin leaned over and kissed her lightly between the breasts, murmuring something about what beautiful eyes she had. Miss Foley was most amused, but I saw her eyes narrow a trifle.

The suite was ablaze with lights, and Rick's thistle-thatched head was bent over the bar when we arrived. There is a certain integrity in being as plain looking as Rick Walton. People trust you, somehow. He came to greet us with a good deal of dignity, and you felt that he was really glad to see you. His sharp face was eager and interested, and he met the girls, whom he already knew, with breeding in his gesture and speech. It was not the bluff heartiness of lawyers or the handrubbing affability that ministers have. It was, I think, sincerity. When we had done with the preliminary skirmishes, we sat down and had a drink. Jarvis and I had ours straight; the rest were mixed.

The group of us, locked behind paneled doors and brocade curtains in an eyrie over the streets of Fort Worth, was conscious of knowing how to react conventionally under given situations, and of being a scrubbed and presentable segment of country-club Christianity. We were all comforted by the unspoken realization, and so we talked earnestly, said nothing, and drank our drinks. The girls had their legs crossed.

Things changed sharply in the next two hours. The bar was appreciably depleted, and our tongues were loosened. Smoke trailed in long festoons across the place, and the rugs were torn back for dancing. The girls didn't have their legs crossed. Miss Foley was sitting in a deep leather chair, and Jarvis was sitting beneath her.

"You can't beat good Scotch!" she said, and flung her head restlessly.

Cavin kissed her. "Of course you can't," he murmured. "It will beat you every time," and he put his hand lightly, testingly, on her hip.

Rick and his date were in the far corner. She was playing the piano, and Rick was not as tidy as he had been. He was draped across the top of the piano, and both hands were clutched in his bristling thatch of hair. Again and again he made Dorothy play "Poor Little Glad Rag Doll," as though that melancholy ballad satisfied some deep hungering.

Out on the terrace, Lucille and I leaned on the ledge and watched the lights. They spread out fanwise before us, like skeins of yellowed stars flung down riotously over the dark shoulder of the prairie. She was standing in front of me. Very close. We were pleased to be inquisitive as to the status quo behind the glimmering lights, and she pointed suddenly.

"A plumber lives there," she announced. "He lost two fingers in the battle of the Marne, and Agatha, his wife, is big with child as she sleeps beside him . . ."

"A thought," I said from behind her, "and a good idea for a song. To be called 'The Pregnant Woman and the Plumber.'"

"I think it's been done." She turned around.

"If you mean impregnation," I said, "it certainly has."

The wind whispered and we listened to it in silence for a moment, and then I put my hands on her, lightly. The dress was tight on her body; its tautness was sleek under my fingers. Her breasts made firm mounds under the material, and the open palms of my hands went down to her hips, but in full flight they were stayed and I looked out over the lights again. Her voice was a trifle mocking in the darkness.

"Gentleman discovers lady has on no lingerie, but does not comment. Are you shocked?"

The wind flowed cool over the high parapet of the hotel. I gave her a cigarette and took one myself. When I lighted them, my hands were unsteady. "I am not particularly shocked," I said, "but I am interested as all get out."

I could hardly see her face, but she was smiling and then both of us were smiling. It was a night of many stars. I was so thankful for the moment that I did not touch her again. It was a moment brittle as glass.

"We don't have much," I said. "No peg to hang our faith on, but this time, now, might be something bright and shining in the sombre catacombs of the confusion we will eventually know. If it is right, it can be as right as wheat rippling in wind or as well understood as a blow in the face . . ." I bent down and kissed her, but not too hard. "It can be the frolic of dirty, curious little children or it can be a finer thing. It can be the best argument for mankind."

It was an old routine, and I was angered suddenly that I didn't have something better to say to her. Standing in the high place with the wind in my eyes and her breasts rising and falling beneath black ruffles, I knew myself for a very threadbare Galahad, but it was all I could give.

She was quiet for a long time, and when she raised her head, her eyes were pooled in emotion. I stood watching her, making my plans and locating the necessary furniture in the suite behind us, but I felt sick inside. It was too easy and I damned the wind and its insistent small applause around the corner of the building.

She put her hands up to her eyes, and I gave her a clean handkerchief. Then I stood there with the whiskey burning in me and the wind rocking me, and when she was through dabbing at her eyes, she kissed me hungrily.

"Want a drink?" I asked.

"But of course." Her hands went up to her hair in that age-old gesture of arrangement. "Of course," she repeated. "I like it better than fried chicken," and as we turned toward the tall French doors I gauged her from her thin shoulders down to the trim buttocks.

The progress of parties where people are drinking can be traced definitely by the character of the jokes that are told at succeeding intervals. Our party went the same way, and we wound into the morning hours becoming less inhibited all the time. Previously we had been regaled with interesting little lascivious bits from the girls, who had gotten them from their schools in the East.

It is a contention of mine that finishing schools must have a course in bawdiness of speech, a sort of complement to good posture, French, and horseback riding, for I have heard some septic anecdotes pass the lips of the young girls. They must receive a fulsome education which I missed in my schools and in the oil fields.

At any rate, we heard a great many of these items, some clever and some distinguished by extreme filth. Cavin grew restless during the telling of them, and when a moment of silence came, he fingered his tie and looked at the ceiling.

He knew a joke too, and he told it slowly, almost insultingly, flicking it off his tongue at us. His joke was a deliberate mace. It was a carefully descriptive anecdote about a man making love to a woman who had been dead three days, a woman who was occupied by maggots. Silence was in the room after he finished it. Nobody even smiled, and a moment of torpor clutched us all.

There were no more jokes. Rick made a strangling sound and the girls seemed to be transfixed, staring at Cavin, but his face was impassive. Miss Foley was perplexed.

"That's not very funny," she said hesitantly.

Jarvis looked at her. A bottle was tilted in his hand. "Honey," he said, "it didn't have to be," but he missed her with that one too, and Rick crossed the room and switched on some savage dance music. The beat of it tugged at us, and Rick threw back his head and howled.

"Oh me, but it's a drunk bitch out tonight . . ." he shouted.

Miss Foley put up one finger and hitched her hips across the room. "Yeah, man!" she moaned, with a sliding inflection. I thought it was rather inept, but about that time Lucille put her hand in mine and we danced.

Dancing has long been a custom. With Lucille it was an elusive promise. The flat planes of her hips and the disturbing pressure of her breasts came alive in music; they were the very heart of the thing the music was calling up. I said to myself that I was going to enjoy this night, and glee dodged like a cavorting imp back of my eyes.

I kissed her lightly, held so, and she clung to me. Her hand moved over my back, and her shoulders were smooth to my encircling arm. I am not a good dancer but I can think and I can feel, and I was sore beset. Under and over the strident beckoning of the melody, the touch of her body, felt all along mine, did promise bliss and we whirled until our legs entwined.

Because I had been drinking and because I had the rawness of sensibility that comes at certain times to all who know the bowl, I came even closer to her and remembered all the bright eyes and warm hands that had touched me, all the good things caught in a mesh of memory.

The music stopped and we came to a halt and someone shouted at us, but I didn't get the sense of it. All I knew was that the blood was pounding at my wrists and temples, and so I looked down at her.

"I wish I had not had a drink," I said, and lied most grievously. "I wish that you and I were not here . . ."

Rick heard me and was nettled. "Do not be detained," he said.

I was still looking at her. "Tell me," I went on, "is there really balm in Gilead?"

Her head was down. "Oh, for God's sake, please stop it," she whispered, and then I turned and led her out of the room into another room. The door shut softly behind us, and I remember wondering how the recoil mechanism worked.

It was dark in the room. Reflections from the lights on the street below cast up a pale fire through the windows, but it was not light enough to see well. Her hand was in mine, and I lifted her up on the bed and lay down beside her.

Then I made no move, staring at the ceiling and listening to the blood yammer up and down my veins. I was like that when she kissed me. Her breath was tainted by drinking; her lips were loose and pendulous. She was leaning over me, and when her lips found mine, the pressure of them slithered over my mouth and pulled at my hips with unbidden strings. My hands found her breasts and the finding was sweet to the fingertips.

I touched her body, gently at first, savoring anticipation as against the fullness of her yielding, and far back in my head the cold logical voice whispered "she's a gone goose; easy does it . . ." and I began to talk.

What I said, what urgency gave me wit to say, I will not ever know, but suddenly her naked breasts were hot against my face and my touch became more harsh. I heaved up and was encased in the warm rapture that is beyond belief. She was pliant and tumultuous; she rolled like a willow stricken by heavy winds, and the night clanged by outside, fully sufficient to its ends. For that interim, we were held scorching out among the stars and infinity trickled by us with a thin roar. But the clinical voice was still in my head, telling me to ask her if she believed in God or if she had a good thing in the fifth at Rockingham.

"Now!" she cried in a smothered voice, and her back arched sharply. "Now!" she cried, and rolled like a tree shedding rich fruit. I was transfixed and she beneath me. Locked together, we shuddered madly, stricken by the oldest ague in the world, and then I did not need her.

I not only did not need her. The musty smell of whiskey and the warm woman smell wreathed up and confused me, so that I could not stand to be near her. I came off the bed and started for the door. Then I remembered my cigarettes, and came back to get them. I lighted two and handed one to her. Her face was drawn in the oval of flame my cupped hands held. She looked at me without smiling.

"Was there," she asked quietly, "balm in Gilead?"

I was shaking all over; I shoved the cigarettes in my pocket and struck out for the door. Some indefinable sickness was ripping me.

"I'll be back in a minute," I said, and winced when the light from the other room slashed into my eyes.

10

ABOUT three o'clock, Cavin and I took our dates home. We called down, ordered the car, and then sailed out through the hall and into the elevator. I do not exaggerate when I say we sailed. Rick's date, Dorothy Barney, wouldn't leave. She was in the bedroom with Rick, and most adamant.

"I won't even consider it," she shouted, when I mentioned going home, and Rick grinned furtively, his hair bristling straight up.

"You must have hidden charms, Mr. Walton," I said, and looked down at him. His arms were folded under his head.

"Didn't mean to hide anything," he caroled, and grinned again.

"Why don't you start a charm school," I asked, "and hold little Saturday afternoon classes?"

Miss Barney twisted on the bed and rumpled him lovingly.

"He is the most charming and the sweetest boy in all creation," she announced, and her face cracked halfway open as she bent to kiss him. Over her shoulder, Rick's eyes were wise and knowing, so I went out of the room and joined the others.

Not much was said on the way home. Jarvis was permeated with whiskey, and any remark at all drew blasphemy of unbelievable stridence from him. The girls were silent, and I was deeply engrossed in driving the car. It was no small task. We went catapulting through the silent streets, and only good fortune kept someone from coming out of a side road, else there would have been a gentle rain of parts and people.

I kissed Lucille at the door of her home, and asked her to give me a date for the Tonto Club Dance. Her eyelashes were wet but she gave me the date, and I told her she would like married life if she married the right people. It was just something I threw in for effect, like a set of dishes, but it shook her and she clung to me. I wanted to be gone. I disentangled her arms and kissed her again.

"Next Tuesday at nine," I said. She echoed me and stepped through the door. Jarvis and his date were not speaking, and we proceeded in silence to her door. He wouldn't get out and go up with her, so I had to. He was muttering in the back seat as I got out, but I couldn't cope with it. At the door I kissed her, too, but her fervor surprised me. We did it again, more carefully.

Jarvis maintained his silence on the way to town. I was driving entirely too fast, and was nearly there when he spoke for the first time.

"How was it?" There was a slur in his voice.

I was properly ignorant. "How was what?"

"Oh, quit that goddamned stalling, how was Blenheim?"

I miraculously avoided a milk truck and straightened out.

"You talk like a man with a solid mahogany head," I told him slowly, and made another corner with the tires screaming.

He said no word; his eyes were glazed and impenetrable. Then he twisted his shoulders, sniffed, and spoke with drunken solemnity.

"I'm going to cut myself in on that," he said.

It was a straight road and I poured the cooking oil to her; we went along with considerable velocity.

"If you do," I answered, "I am going to break your back and kick your brains out . . . ," and then the battle lines were drawn and we went smashing down the empty street.

Rick was eating a filet mignon when we got back. When I enquired where the lady was, he jerked a thumb toward the bathroom and continued his munching. It was nearly five o'clock, and I mentioned something about going home.

"In due time," he said. "Everything in due time, Jimble."

Jarvis was sluicing down some whiskey that could not possibly get him any more intoxicated, and I had to fight my head to keep standing up. I got angry.

"Damn it, Rick," I shouted, "time is wasting. It'll be broad daylight in an hour. Call this grubworm out and let's us go home."

Walton gobbled on the filet. He whinnied with disapproval, his mouth full. "You are shouting, Jimble," he coughed out. "You are creating undue noise and commotion. All in good time." He looked up and spread his hands, palms flat. His mouth was greasy. "The Lord giveth," he said, "and the Lord, Bless His Holy Name, taketh away . . ."

A bellboy came in and Rick signed the ticket.

"Money," he said to me, "give this boy alms in the name of Jehovah."

What I had was a half dollar, and I relinquished it with some reluctance. The boy went out, knuckling his head, and I got mad again.

"Now Rick . . ." I began, and was forming an excoriation on my tongue when a rude battering began to take place on the door. The clamor was considerable, and Rick stopped eating to lend an ear.

"Who is it?" he called.

A robust voice answered him. "Open this goddamned door," it said, and since I am an intuitive fellow, I went across the room, jerked Cavin out of his chair, and pulled him into a closet near the door of the suite. He sagged considerably, but he stood up. I heard Rick leave the table on bare feet, and a few seconds later, the outside door of the suite splintered and crashed open. Several people trampled into the room and began to mill around; somebody said that they were going to kill somebody deader than hell, and then an even greater commotion broke loose. It was hard to hear all they were saying because I had to keep Jarvis muzzled, but the angry voices buzzed on outside and once I heard Dorothy crying. After a time the noises subsided and footfalls faded out into the hall. When I had waited awhile, I stepped out, pulling Jarvis with me. The suite was empty and the shattered door was ajar, so I closed it as well as I could and took a bottle out of Cavin's hands.

"Jarvis," I said, "the fat is in the fire. That noise was Dotty's old man, and he was vexed."

But Jarvis was out of the ken of mortal reckoning.

"Des'late," he gibbered, his handsome face twisting. "Think I will have a big-ass cry. Want Lucille. Hell 'ith Rick, want Lucille . . ."

I shoved him over onto the sofa. He fell without resistance, and he did not move after he had fallen. I wondered where Rick was, and searched the three rooms, but he wasn't in any of them. The last time I had seen him, when he was eating, he had been wearing only a pair of shorts, but none of his clothes were about. That he had been a bird of passage, I could easily deduce, but just what had been his passage and whether or not it had been disputed, preyed on my mind. I stood there swaying, trying to figure it out, but I was wound too tight, and, flopping down beside Jarvis, I sought surcease of sleep.

Sunlight was slanting through the Venetian blinds when I awoke. Jarvis was beside me on the couch, and his wavy black hair was rumpled. A pillow was riding on the back of his neck, and he wafted up an irregular snoring. He didn't look so good.

When I reached for the phone, my fingers went fluctuating out like each one had a little motor in it. I withdrew my hand and regarded it at some length. It was that bad. Finally I put both hands out and lifted the phone from its cradle. When my number answered, I affected a casual tone. It was my mother, and I told her who it was, just in case she didn't recognize the voice. Her answer was oracular.

"You'll find out someday," she said distinctly, "that some people can drink and get away with it. You can't."

"Okay." She was right, but that didn't help my head any. "Spare me the theorizing," I said. I felt like hell and dry heat waves were pulsing through my face. "By the way, Rick hasn't called me yet, has he?"

"Just a minute," she answered, and put the phone down. I thought she was going after a number, but in a minute, Rick's voice came over the wire.

"Jimble?" he whispered, and there was great anxiety in it.

"Yes?"

"Where are you?"

"What difference does it make," I bellowed, "I'd feel just as bad anyplace else."

He was breathless with fright, and he sounded like he had crept up into the phone.

"Now don't start that damned gaggin'," he said, "because the jam is on. Barney's old man busted in the door last night with two other guys. He says he is going to kill me plumb out of hand."

He stopped then, and I could hear him breathing.

"How did you get away?"

He was scared to death. "I jumped," he quavered, "jumped from that terrace down to the eighteenth floor porch."

I was startled. “But that’s thirty feet or more.”

He laughed for the first time. “It didn’t take but a second,” he said.

“What about your clothes?”

“Oh,” he said, “I threw the pants out first and jumped into them. The rest I just carried along and put on in the taxicab, on the way to your house.”

Jarvis came up back of my elbow and took the cigarette from between my fingers. He was yawning distastefully and grimacing. Rick’s voice crackled in the receiver again.

“Old man Barney’s going to kill you too,” he said, and then I was wide awake. I told Rick to stay there, that we would be out immediately, and then I got up and took a cold shower. As I was drying off, I told Jarvis the situation but he was not much help.

“I don’t care,” he said bitterly, “I don’t care if both of you get gunned to death. I just plain goddamned don’t care . . .”

I thought him rather callous to speak of his chums in such a fashion, but I don’t imagine he did care. He dressed slowly, pausing to curse when he saw that the pocket on his new jacket had been ripped. He was sulphuric about it all the way down to the lobby. Our taxi had just pulled up and we were entering it when Rick’s father came out of the hotel and called to me.

After telling Jarvis to go home, I slammed the cab door and turned around. In silence Mr. Walton and I paced back across the lobby and rode up to the suite. Four men were there, and I wondered how Cavin and I had missed them coming down.

Three of the men I knew; one of them was Rick’s uncle who owned the hotel, the smooth-jowled one with the brisk air was a notable criminal lawyer, and the balding little man with the pig eyes was a leading banker. When the introductions were performed, I found out that the other one was Chief of City Detectives. All in all, it was a noteworthy conclave, and they were all staring at me. I returned their gaze, but the whole cotton crop of the South was in my mouth.

"Gentlemen," I said, "I am your servant, but foolishly, I got drunk last night, and if I don't get a Bromo-Seltzer I will start plucking the violets from the wall paper."

Nobody moved a muscle. Everybody was rich except the detective, and he was tough, which is a stage of richness. Mr. Walton picked up the phone and ordered a double Bromo. It was a dubious compliment, and when he was through, he leaned forward.

"Now, Jimble," he said, "about this girl Barney."

I was thankful that I had taken Lucille home early enough. Outside the hotel, it was noon, and I could hear a shrill voice piping murder in the streets, could feel that all the clerks were crowding out of their offices to shoot frayed cuffs at blue-plate specials. Somewhere, on one of the ledges, a bird ignorant of disaster trebled up a syrupy song as I leaned forward and began to tell the earnest gentlemen what I knew about this girl Barney.

11

THE gentlemen were of several minds. The banker said to buy the girl off as cheaply as possible. The lawyer, however, was dubious of this, and Rick's uncle thought perhaps there had better be a marriage and quick divorce. The detective, a man named Lester, was a free soul. He unbuttoned his coat elaborately, and the butt of his holstered gun was obvious as an extra leg.

"Now Mr. Walton," he mused slowly, "I don't know the situation, but if this Barney guy wants to kill somebody, maybe I ought to go out and see him. Of course, I'd be countin' on you to see me through, but it wouldn't be no job to chill him."

The gentlemen rocked like chairs. Banker Lightner was most upset, and Mr. Walton whinnied reproachfully and shook his head. They all got very busy telling Lester to keep his gun silent.

"Only as the last resort," finished off Drummond, the criminal lawyer, "absolutely only as a last resort."

He was serving his capacity, and his voice was still lingering in the air when the telephone jangled. Mr. Walton answered it, and his face was grim as he hung up.

"Barney was downstairs a few minutes ago," he said, "and offered one of the bellboys a hundred dollars to tell him where we were hiding Rick. When the boy ducked in and told the desk man, Barney left."

Lester hitched in his chair. "I can go right down and get him," he said.

"No!" Mr. Walton was emphatic. For all his posturings and sharp practice dealings, his brow was furrowed by an honest regard for Rick's safety. He spoke again into the phone, telling the desk to let him know if Barney came back. When he turned to us, he was simple in speech.

"I've got money," he said. "I don't care what happens, but I don't want my boy to get hurt."

There was no subterfuge in it. He had offered up what was to him the greatest thing in life. What he spoke was an apparent truth, and we all stared at him as if he had uncovered an ancient magic. Banker Lightner toyed with his glasses absently. I suppose he was computing the interest rate on fidelity, and the bird was still splitting his throat outside the window. It was the lawyer, as usual, who brought the bad news.

"Jimble," he began sonorously, and pierced me with his gaze. I had seen too many lawyers. It was court room stuff. "Jimble," he rumbled, "would you be afraid to go out and see Barney?"

The sunlight in the room was heavy moted, and I stared at the conference of capitalists. They were all staring back at me.

"Mr. Drummond," I asked him suddenly, "would you be afraid to go out and see Barney?"

He was taken aback. He fumbled with his cigar.

"No bearing," he muttered, "no bearing on the case at all . . ."

He was still in the deep throes of expostulation when I got up. I didn't like the men. I didn't like the things they stood for. I didn't like the detective that offered to go out and kill a man because he knew Walton and the others could get him out of it easily. I didn't like the pudgy banker. All I could see in his eyes was seven percent. I put my topcoat over my arm and creased my hat. I creased it because it was uncreased.

"I'll go out and see him," I said slowly, "but understand, it won't be because of any of you. I'll go out to see him for Rick. I don't give a damn about the rest of it."

The gentlemen nodded in chorus, and all of a sudden I knew that they were afraid, that the banker's expensive facade had sheltered him and softened him until he was afraid, and that the lawyer was juggling advantageous statutes in his head but that on no account would he go out and see Mr. Barney. Only for the detective did I have any semblance of respect. He, at least, was willing to go out and put a few slugs into the man. I picked up my cigarettes and started out. Mr. Walton said that they would be waiting to hear from me, and did I want a squad car to follow me out? I told him no, and went out the door wondering how the Americans had ever beaten the British.

It was bright outside, and I was about to call a cab when I remembered that my car was parked in the garage next to the hotel. I figured out that it would be a waste of money to use a cab. As I was driving away, I flipped on the radio. A tenor who seemed to be in actual pain was lunging through a song about the moon getting in his eyes. My hands were clammy, my breath was bad, and a nerve started jerking in my cheek. I put one hand over it, but it kept throbbing and leaping under my fingers. Inwardly, I took a vote to see if I was scared, and it wasn't even close. I lost, and when I pulled up before Barney's house, my tongue seemed some inches bigger than the mouth that held it.

The button on the door raised a faint hum in the back of the house, and after a few minutes, a negro girl opened the door. A circular white cap was on her fuzzy head.

"I want to see Mr. Barney," I said, but I was lying. I didn't really want to see Mr. Barney.

She opened the door and motioned me into the living room. It was a long room with massy furniture and a used look. The low ceiling was beamed and dark. It was a room that people had lived in, and I sat down in one of the big chairs and lighted a cigarette, a process requiring two hands. Sunlight slanted through the draped windows and flung bars of gold across the rug. Somewhere in the house, subdued laughter welled up and was smothered by a closing door. I was immeasurably cheered; I hoped that everyone would be laughing, but I could not stop wondering where Mr. Barney was. Sitting there, I began to think about Lucille, and memory put its crawling touch on the back of my neck. I was absorbed with the reflection and did not consciously know when the figure came to stand in the door.

It was Mr. Barney. He was in the doorway watching me. His thin face was intent, and his stance was very straight, feet close together. Because he was standing where a shaft of sunlight hit him, I could see that his eyes were darkly red veined. He wore only a shirt and pants, with leather slippers on his feet, but the gun on his hip made him look ridiculously overdressed to me. He was a rich man, but he had come up the hard way, out of the ranks of oil field labor. I had seen him before, at the club with Warstler, but I had not particularly noticed him.

"Damn you," he said, not moving. "So you're one of them."

"Yes." I got up. "I guess I'm one of them."

He came into the room a little way and put both hands on his face, as though rubbing might pull the tension out of it. He savaged his face with both hands.

"I'll kill this Rick Walton," he said.

"Do you think that will help any?" I was still standing up and I was taller than he was.

"Makes no difference," he went on in a calm voice. "He took my daughter to his hotel and got her drunk and violated her like a common whore. When I find him, and I'll find him, he will be dead before the news can get to God."

He was a man who knew his own mind. I tried another tack, but it was a mistake.

"I was there all the time, Mr. Barney," I said, "and I'm sure he didn't touch her."

He looked straight at me, as if for the first time.

"That's right," he mused, "you were there all the time. Maybe you got this party up. I know you took her down there in your car. Maybe you're the main instigator in this business of taking girls down there and cracking them."

He rocked back on his heels, and stared at me out of those heavily blood-shot eyes.

"I think maybe I ought to kill you too," he went on, "and then him and then her. Maybe I just ought to kill the whole kit and caboodle of you and stop all this crap."

I didn't say anything because I felt that my field was limited. If he had been shouting I wouldn't have worried so much, but he was talking calmly and quietly, as if he were thinking of having the trees in his yard disinfected. A strained smile fought across his mouth.

"Yessir," he said, "maybe I ought to kill the whole bunch, beginning with you." He was looking at me, and I was wishing he wouldn't smile so strangely.

Somebody else must have said it, but it came out of my mouth. Surely I didn't say it, because I am smarter than that, but there it was, hanging in the room . . .

"Well, I am right here and you've got the gun."

The silence was long and tremendous. A rivulet of sweat started out of my left sideburn and trickled agonizingly down my cheek. I would have given a great deal to scratch it, but I didn't. I watched Mr. Barney.

"What would you do?" he asked softly, "if I started to shoot you?"

He was still smiling that odd smile, and a note of academic interest was in his voice. I didn't even want to talk about it so I levelled with him.

"Mr. Barney," I stammered, the words tumbling out, "I would start spinning like a little red top."

My arms were flexed and I shifted on the rug. The maid passed by the door, stopped, and went back out of sight. I knew it was the maid because the white cap blurred in the corner of my eye. It was all the attention I could give her because I was still watching Mr. Barney, and fear was turning turgidly in my belly. I was wondering if he could hear the loud pound of my heart when he turned away abruptly and flopped into a chair.

He didn't sit down. From a standing position, he fell into the chair and his head rolled, he expelled his breath sharply, and tension flowed out of him like water from a broken bowl. He was turned away from me, sitting with his legs crossed, and in the silence he began to cry. Quietly and heavily. His shoulders shook under the weight of his grief, and I reached up and flipped the sweat from my face, listening to the choking sound.

Into my mind, without warning, there came an understanding that had not been there before. Thirty seconds ago, I had been afraid that he was going to kill me, but now, with that danger gone, I looked down on his shaking shoulders and realized that he was right, that the gun on his hip and the terrible, strained calm in his voice were the only defenses he had as a wronged man. It was a normal reaction to the treatment we had given his daughter. I mopped my face, listened to his dry sobbing, and thought of Dorothy, his girl, growing up in that house. I tried to understand what she would be like reading in the big chairs and playing in the yard and going away to school to absorb dubious culture and a spirited stock of cliches while he watched her grow up, under his guidance. She was something he had worked for, loved, and seen come alive as a projection of his personality. I tried to understand it. It was a concept of responsibility, viewed like that, which I had never thought of before. Nobody had taught it to me, but I was not alone in my ignorance.

"Mr. Barney," I began, trying to let him know, not stopping to think that you cannot talk about those things. I just called his name and stopped; it was a stupid thing to do.

"Get out," he said wearily, in a voice washed clean of emotion.

I walked toward the door.

"I'll kill Rick Walton," he said doggedly, and I opened the door and stepped out into the full sunlight.

My head was pounding and I felt as though I wanted to vomit, but I fought my stomach and started to drive away. The gear meshed under my hand, and as the car gathered speed, I was pondering the terrible things that people can do to each other.

The conclave was still sitting when I got back. They were around the table, all smoking cigars that fitted their faces perfectly. The detective had taken his coat off, but that was the only change. They glanced up when I came in, and Mr. Walton came over and shook hands with me.

"What luck?" he asked.

The rest of them were rared back behind a barrage of filmy smoke. The banker licked what lips he had, and Lawyer Drummond cracked his knuckles methodically. Rick's Uncle Harry rubbed his bald pate, and Lester flipped a coin from hand to hand.

"He was pretty upset," I said. "He wanted to kill all three of us."

"Why, in heaven's name?" queried Lightner, the banker. He could see no profit in such random slaughter and he laced his fingers together nervously.

I stared out the window. "He said it might stop all this crap." And then I told them the rest of it, neglecting to say that Barney had broken down. I didn't think that was any of their business. When I came to the part about Barney knocking me off too, maybe, Lightner got halfway out of his chair. His little eyes were shining, and his lips were wet where he had licked them.

"What did he do then?" he whispered, and I was irrationally angered.

The little pot-bellied man was tense as a hunting dog, and I revolted against playing stooge to his vicarious adventurings.

"He shot me eleven times," I said simply, and watched incredulity drain into and out of his eyes. He cleared his throat and sucked moistly on the cigar as he sat back down. Mr. Walton's tone was placating.

"Now, Jimble," he intoned, "this is a serious affair."

Just as if I didn't know it was a serious thing, hadn't seen the serious stare in the muzzle of Barney's gun. But I still didn't tell them about the man crying, and, but for Rick, I don't know whose side I would have been on.

When I was through, Mr. Walton called Rick, talked to him shortly, and sent Lester out to my house in a squad car. After the detective had left, I went into the bathroom and took another shower, letting the cold water sting down over me. Now that I had slowed down, the hangover put its fangs into me with a vengeance. The cold water helped some, and I was shivering on the mat, buffing up my body with a towel, when Rick came into the suite. He was still afraid; I could tell that when he spoke.

"Yes sir," he said, very low. There was a tremor in his voice, and I stepped out into the other room with a towel wrapped around my hips. Rick looked across at me, and a wraith of a smile passed over his face.

"Bad luck, Rick-tick," I said, and he replied that it was a miracle of understatement. "In case it wasn't as good as you had expected it to be," I went on, "you were certainly cheated."

The other men laughed shortly and indulgently, except the detective, who nearly knocked himself out. The joke wasn't that humorous, and it explained why he was a detective. But I didn't care about them anyway, and I got another smile out of Rick. Mr. Walton came over and put an arm around his son's shoulders.

"Lester, here, is going to take you out to the ranch," he said, "and you're going to stay out there until this thing blows over."

He took a gun out of his pocket and handed it to Rick, who was not a great one for firearms. He juggled the pistol nervously, and finally dropped it into his coat pocket.

Three more detectives came in and stood across from us, their hats in hand. It was turning out to be quite an entourage. They were all big leatherfaced men with windwrinkled eyes, and looked competent but not too smart. They beamed on Rick with a fraternal air, as though they too, to the last man, had been visited by the flame at one time or another. Indubitably, there was a bond, and things got right cozy at the last.

"Don't worry, Mr. Walton," said Lester, big hat in his hand, "the boy will be all right."

He put on his hat, and while I was shaking hands with Rick, Mr. Walton pulled out a roll of bills that looked like a fistful of bay leaves with gland trouble. Part of it he gave to Rick, and the rest he handed to Lester, who palmed it with a practiced twist. The rest of the men shook hands with Rick.

"Remember not to fire," I said, "until you see the whites of their thighs," and young Rick went out of the room grinning and well protected.

The detectives were laughing heartily; their mirth came back down the hall to us, but the men left behind didn't find the remark very amusing, for which I could not blame them. Mr. Walton said that I had better keep in touch with him, that Barney probably wouldn't do anything, but that you never could tell. I admitted that you never could tell. It was the only thing open to me. Then they all went out and I massaged my scalp. I didn't think it would do much good, but I couldn't give up entirely. While I was knuckling my head, the telephone rang and Bradley's voice husked over it.

"What in the name of God is going on?" he asked. "Cavin is drunk again, or yet, and tellin' the damndest tales I ever heard."

"True," I said, "all true, but tell Cavin to shut up." I told Fred the whole story, and at the end of every sentence, he said "Jesus" or "Jesus Christ."

After he had hung up, the phone rang again and a voice said that if I wished the suite for another day, would I please register. I said that I would not want the suite any more just yet. There was a pause on the line.

"To whom shall I charge the long distance calls made last night?"

I didn't remember the calls, but I could see how it might have happened.

"Just charge them to publicity," I said, and put the phone down. My shirt smelled like the harness off an industrious mule, but I pulled it on and went out, stopping only to notice the number of the suite. As I waited for the elevator, I listed it under the Department of Places To Be Avoided in the Future. There were beavers in my brains, and I said something about it to the elevator boy, but he was laconic and gloomy. As he opened the door at the lobby level, he turned toward me.

"Cripes and Apostles," he said, "some on horseback."

I smiled pleasantly, got out, and was halfway through the lobby when the thought of it hit me. His elevator was gone, but I waited until it came back down.

"I beg your pardon," I said, "but what was it you told me just now?"

He shook his head sorrowfully. "Cripes," he repeated, "and Apostles, some on horseback."

"I see." But I didn't see. I repeated it after him, several times. "What made you say it?"

He shrugged and his cadaverous face twisted. "Oh, I don't know," he answered. "They just come to me . . ."

His buzzer sounded, a sharp imperative sound, and he closed the elevator door.

I went outside and tested it on the doorman. He was strutting up and down, a burly negro resplendent in gold braid. He stopped and listened to me with his shoulders thrown back, and his black face twisted in thought.

"You cain't never tell," he said hoarsely, and, after blinking in the sunlight for a moment, I got in my car and drove away.

12

A DELAYED hangover is a cruel affliction. I am not familiar with the quantitative theory of alcohol absorption, hence I cannot explain the dogmas involved, but when a man drinks long enough, drinks in vain combat against the inevitable hour of reckoning, he will reach and pass the saturation point and arrive finally at that dismal outpost of intoxication where whiskey rims his eyes, leaves his mouth trembling, and puts vague and tricky wonder in his head. This sensation of wonder is most dangerous of all, for it will lead perilous close to the shadow line where buffoons dance eternally in greenish twilights and the dead are not dead and one can walk upon the water. It is a concomitant of these periods of suspension after extreme drunkenness that newsboys become potential presidents, and one wishes to take them home, clean and clothe them, and send them off to be Rhodes scholars and great characters in history. But all newsboys do not have presidential calibre, as the grandeurs of hangover fever will lead us to believe, and one must be wary. Then too, moments come that bring a swift descent into the abyss, where life in toto is unadulterated hell.

It was with knowledge of these matters that I awoke in the afternoon after Rick Walton's precipitate departure from town. I came awake without warning and found myself staring at the grim visage of the tarpon hanging on my wall. The supercilious smirk graven on that piscatorial head did not rouse my spirits any, and I thrust my body stiffly along under the sheets, accounting for legs and arms. I was conscious of the crusty feel of my eyelids, as though a fine dust had caked there, and a languorous, almost painful aching threaded through my whole body. A nerve was jerking fitfully in my right cheek, and distaste for the world went hammering through my mind as I heaved up and stared at myself in the long mirror on the closet door.

Reddened eyes stared back at me without enthusiasm. Excess had etched its wavering warnings along my chin, and the sacs of my eyes were dark and puffed. I halfheartedly dodged the fellow in the mirror a few times, but soon gave it up, for he was as fast as I was. Then, for awhile, I just sat in the middle of the bed listening to the construction work being carried on in my head. Something big was being built; I could tell that, and when I remembered where the bottle was cached, I tiptoed over to the bookshelf for it.

There was a drink left, but the smell came up out of the bottle and thonged at my stomach. My whole body tightened convulsively and jerked in protest, so I put the bottle down and lighted a cigarette. The first acrid smoke made my head whirl; it forced me to hang on to the bedpost. But things grew better after a few minutes and I took the drink, flopped back on the bed, and waited for the whiskey to build its firm fire.

A pleasant glow spread in the stomach, like water colors running on a blotter, and the glow mantled upward toward the brain. I lay there savoring it and wondering whether or not to go down and get some breakfast. I thought to myself that I would not bother with the stairs, just step right down out of the window and conserve my strength. The idea was faulty, and, after consideration, I realized it, so I put on a robe and inched down the stairs.

Pearl was dusting in the living room, dusting to swing time, and she flirted the oiled rag like a stout black dervish. I jigged into the room with one finger raised.

"Good mornin', good mornin', a brand new day is dawning . . ." I caroled, and Pearl gave the piano a parting slap and took up the chorus.

"A happy, carefree, gay good mornin' to you . . ."

"And to you, Pearl," I said gravely. "Have you seen my brains around here?"

"Brains?" Her bulldog face was puzzled. "Oh, Mr. Jimble, you is foolin'."

"I certainly are not," I said. "I have lost all my brains, Pearl."

She was undecided.

"Land's sake," she murmured.

"Have you seen them in your matutinal peregrinations?"

She smiled broadly and shook her kinky thatch. "Nawsir, but I kin fix you a potion for that achin' head," she announced, with the air of one who has cut a Gordian knot. I bowed low.

"Madame, I shall count it no little favor," I said, and she cackled heartily and went waddling back to the kitchen.

Sunlight slanted through the figured lace curtains and dappled the red rug. Through the blinds, I could see some women standing on the fifth tee. As I watched, with my hands thrust into the pockets of the dressing gown, the lady golfers waggled their rumps one after the other, and lunged at the ball. The thought came to me that the object ball should be larger for the girls, say about grapefruit size. Turning the proposition over in my mind, I watched the feminine foursome waver through their stiff arcs and strike out down the fairway. I lighted another cigarette and had taken three drags from it when the telephone rang.

It was for me. An earnest young lady named Wilkins, calling for the Little Theatre, informed me that the next play was to be "The Road to Rome," and would I play the part of a Carthaginian corporal?

"It is not a large part," gushed Miss Wilkins, "but something really fine could be done with it."

"You mean I could steal the show?" I enquired.

There was a pause on the line.

"Well, as to that I'm not sure," answered Miss Wilkins, finally and crisply. She was a trifle offended. "After all, we have Hightower doing the lead . . ."

"Probably run until the end of time. What does a corporal have to do?"

Miss Wilkins wasn't finding any civic spirit, and it hurt her. She wavered uncertainly, "Oh, I don't know. You just say your lines . . ."

Pearl brought me a large glass of tomato juice, and I took a long pull at it.

"One cannot be chary of sympathy for the smaller parts, Miss Wilkins," I said, "but how about a sergeant stint?"

"I'm very sorry," she said briskly. "The other parts have been filled."

I took another drink of the tomato juice. Spices and tart tastes were in it.

"More's the pity," I said, "but as a matter of fact, I'm under contract now. Otherwise I would be flattered."

"Contract?"

"Yes," I said, "I'm playing the fool."

Miss Wilkins was troubled. "Oh, I didn't know. We had so counted on having you. Bob was saying only yesterday that you were exactly what we needed . . ." I didn't call Bob to mind, but she went on.

"This Fool thing, when are you playing it. This month?"

"Yes," I answered. "Undoubtedly this month."

"Next month?"

"In all probability."

Her voice was anguished. "But when will you be through?"

It was a fair question and I considered it gravely, holding the cool glass against my forehead.

"Hard to tell," I said finally, "I have a run of the show contract."

"Oh . . ." She whispered blankly. "But next time maybe?"

"Perhaps," I rejoined, and finished the tomato juice. She said that she wished me luck in "this Fool thing," and I replied that I would undoubtedly need it, and she hung up.

Pearl brought a platter of eggs in and I sat down to them, but without great enthusiasm. I was midway in them, and gazing out over the elms in the backyard when the phone rang again. I took it from the cradle, put it to my ear, and Lucille's voice flowered from the black receiver.

"Good morning!"

"Good morning," I said. "You slept well?"

"Of course. And you?" She was gay. Too gay.

"Exelente. The pure in heart, you know," I answered, puzzled.

"Ah, but that is bound to be hearsay with you," she said archly, and I laughed moderately, wondering when the badinage would cease. When I did not answer she called out my name in a low tone.

"Yes?"

"About last night?" And she waited again, but I would not help her. There was not a drop of Lochinvar in me. "It was all right, wasn't it?"

I reached for a cigarette and found none, so I dispatched Pearl upstairs for some.

"How do you mean, all right?" I queried. "I thought it was exciting."

It was too blunt but it was also too early in the morning. She said nothing for a minute; she was timid and on unfamiliar ground.

"I mean . . . there's no danger, is there?"

"Danger?" I temporized. "But of course not. No. Everything absolutely okay."

"All right."

The words floated over the line. The morning sunlight slanted through the breakfast room windows, and it felt warm and comfortable on my face and arms, but a tremor shook me. She spoke again and as she did, the hangover lifted its vengeance long enough for memory to go smashing through my head.

"I just wondered," she said.

"Weep no more, my lady," I answered, "and remember that we have a date, come Tuesday, for the Tonto dance."

"All right." Her voice sounded lighter and less troubled. "I'll be looking forward to it," she said, and then hung up.

Pearl was thundering around upstairs, and I opened the hall door and asked her where the family was. When I did, she came to lean over the railing of the stairs and her mountainous breasts spilled over laxly. She dropped me a package of cigarettes, and said that "evvabody" was in town someplace, but she didn't know where. I ripped the cellophane off the cigarettes and lighted one, and then I went back into the living room to rest on the couch and pluck at the cords on a floor lamp. I was thinking of Lucille, wondering whether I had been first with her, and if not, I was considering who the scoundrel might have been. It was not logical, but it is what I was doing. The thought process was so discouraging, however, that I finally gave it up and drove over to the Mirrolite office.

Cavin was lying on the cot regarding the ceiling and Fred was patiently numbering a marker, so I sat down and began to read a magazine. Both of them looked at me, grunted shortly, and went back to what they had been doing. It was not the most heart-warming reception I had ever received, but I ignored it entirely and sat there looking at the cartoons in the magazine. We were like that when Buddy Perry pushed the door open and came inside.

"Notice!" he said, fighting an imaginary bull with an imaginary cape, "Mumford's got a job!"

Jarvis went on doing nothing, and Fred lifted his broad face from the wooden panel. His eyes were abstracted.

"A job?" he asked. "Mumford?" The paint brush was poised up by his ear. "You mean a working job?"

Perry made another deft pass with the invisible cape, and his nostrils dilated as the bull went by.

"Yuss," he hissed. "He is now our Mr. Mumford, neckties, socks, shorts, shirts and stuff like that, down to Sack's Store."

Jarvis came up on one elbow.

"My God," he said, "how came him to do a thing like that?"

Perry stood silently, one foot in advance of the other, like a matador accepting the plaudits of the crowd. "Money," he said. "People do things like that for money. It's the only reason."

Jarvis was staring at him, twisting his shoulders under a light crew-necked sweater.

"Pure crap. What does he make?"

Perry whirled in a pas de seul, and that unseen cape settled gently around him. "Wouldn't tell me in the store's office," he said frankly. "Mumford claims twenty a week and commission."

Jarvis lay back down.

"How do you like that?" he asked us generally. "He could always chisel twice that much any week he ever lived."

Bradley chortled. "Ain't it the truth, though?" He bent back over the Mirrolite he was painting, and his mouth twisted as he put the brush down.

The chickens in the pen outside the office clucked drowsily, and sunlight fell through the window and flung a golden fan across the littered floor. It was a somnolent day, and we sat there in the shadowed room considering the fact of Mumford's employment.

"I don't like it," said Jarvis finally. His tone was dubious. "It just doesn't sound right."

Perry was playing the bull again, playing him too close to his body, and he lunged back suddenly, a squarefaced boy pirouetting in the center of the room.

"Close," I said, turning a page of my magazine. "Too close for comfort, that one."

Perry stared at me, his straw-colored thatch motionless above bright eyes.

"Don't worry," he said. "I'm just tiring him out. He'll never get me."

I was doubtful. "Looks like a tough one to me . . ."

"He won't ever in this world get me," promised Perry, and whirled with both hands up as the bull came snorting back at him from the southeast corner of the room. Jarvis got up and pulled on a tan sport coat. Bradley was finishing the sign; he put a few last swipes on it and held it up. Jarvis cocked his head and looked at it critically.

"The Four is lousy," he announced without enthusiasm, and Fred hung the glistening sign on the wall bracket. I could see his lips compress, but he said nothing.

"Watch!" shouted Perry, and came up on his toes for the kill. He had been stepping silently about the room, and now he was ready for the denouement. As we watched, he leaned forward with his body arched and thrust out his arm. Then, as we waited, he twisted the sword in the invisible bull's hump and stood there smiling fiercely.

"Viva!" I cried, coming out of my chair. "Viva Perry!"

He bowed gracefully, and I was still cheering and he was still bowing when Fred yawned and stretched. Jarvis was over in the corner, smouldering about something.

"I don't like it," he said. "Mumford getting a job. Bad business, that." He smoothed back his hair carefully, and his eyes were troubled. "Maybe we oughtta go down and see the Hot Horse."

He looked at me and I shrugged my shoulders. Fred was washing his hands in the bathroom, and he started humming, "what about the Hot Horse, turn te turn, how about the Hot Horse . . ." Perry extricated his sword from the dead bull, and we started toward the door.

"It's all because of the money," said Perry, apologetically. "I have it from him direct that he only did it because of the money."

We climbed into Bradley's brown Buick, and he stomped on the starter and whirled out of the driveway. A truck swerved to avoid hitting us, and the driver cursed fulsomely.

"I don't like it at all," said Jarvis, trailing one hand out of the window.

The store was crowded. Throngs of people were clotted under the high arches of its bastard gothic ceiling, and we pushed through until we came to the Men's Wear section. Mumford was wearing dark glasses, and his slight frame and sharp profile made him look like a growing eaglet. He was behind a counter, fawning on a man in a tweed suit.

The man had three or four neckties in his hand, and we stopped and watched Mumford beam at him. While we watched, with people pushing around us, the Hot Horse kept talking earnestly, and he was in the middle of an oration anent the beauty of those particular pieces of neckwear when he looked up and saw us. After he did, an apprehensive smile flooded his face. He nodded shortly and kept talking, and finally the man put down several dollars. Mumford dropped two ties in a sack, rang the sale up, and we walked over to him.

"Well," he said cheerily, "what goes?"

Jarvis was in front, and he put his hands down on the counter.

"Fine damned thing this is," he said, and started jerking ties out of a box.

Mumford stood in front of us. His smile faded slowly until he was absolutely disconsolate.

"Ain't it a bitch?" he asked.

We agreed that it was, and he stood back of the counter shifting from foot to foot. Jarvis had begun opening more boxes, and Perry was trying on a pair of leather suspenders.

"Now, fellows," pleaded Mumford, "after all, this is my first day."

Jarvis and Perry kept fumbling along the counter, and Mumford kept watching them with a pained look.

"God Almighty," he wailed, "you guys know I'll get stuck for anything you steal." He looked over at me imploringly.

"Silence, clerk," I said. "Fine thing when a few leading citizens can't come into a store like Sacks and not be accused of dishonesty. Call the manager, sirrah!"

The Hot Horse was nervous. He hitched his narrow shoulders and glanced around.

"Jimble," he whispered, "for God's sake don't start that stuff in here." He gazed at me mournfully.

Jarvis and Perry were still rummaging down the counter, and Bradley was across the aisle trying on hats. By the tens and twenties, he was trying hats on his square head.

"I got a little dough," whispered Mumford in my ear. "How about putting a little bet down for me? A fin on Desert Queen in the fifth at Aqueduct. I can't leave here right now, but this baby . . ." He leaned over the counter. "Was fifteen in the morning line. She can win in that company. You can go right down to Massara's and lay it in. Won't take a minute."

"James," I said rebukingly, "not only does Sacks frown upon its employees betting the broomtails, but the horse you speak of has very bad blood lines, and will put up a strenuous snoot for last place. I doubt whether she will be back in the stable by Labor Day."

I had never heard of Desert Queen. Mumford tightened his tie and glanced around.

"It's only two blocks," he said.

"The distance to hell, for you, is shorter than that," I said. "The distance is immaterial. We must consider the principal. Five dollars will buy a little of the old hard, and besides, the horse cannot win."

He was staring at me when a buzzer sounded, and he turned to answer the house phone. He said "Yessir" three times, and hung the phone up.

"I got to go up to the stock room for a minute," he said stiffly. He was still offended because I wouldn't take the bet over for him. "Don't let these bastards take over the whole place."

Then he slipped out from behind the counter and started toward the elevators. On the way, he stopped to say something to Jarvis, who was at the far end of the counter. As soon as he was out of sight, Cavin and Perry sidled back toward me. Perry was humming "The Music Goes Down And Around . . .", and through some oversight, he was still wearing the leather suspenders. Cavin stopped in front of me and stared across the store.

"Well," he said, in the abrupt way which meant that his mind was made up, "I guess we better sell some of this stuff."

I looked at him. "What lines would you like to push?"

"Immaterial," he answered, and walked over into the next aisle.

There he gathered up an armload of floor lamp hoods of all patterns and shapes. A buxom saleswoman hurried over to him, and for a moment they conversed. In the course of it, Jarvis gestured at me and I smiled pleasantly. The woman ducked her head and scurried back up the line to some waiting customers.

Jarvis walked over with his bright burdens and crouched down beside me. He was hidden behind the counter, picking through the articles he had brought across the store. I combed my hair carefully, and looked around.

"Get us a prospect," hissed Jarvis from the floor. "Get 'em in! That's the first rule of merchandising. You can't sell 'em till you've got 'em stopped."

I put my hands down on the counter in a clerkly fashion and looked around some more. "What the hell will you do down there? Are they supposed to come around and lie down by you?"

"No, you stupid ass," he whispered. "You just get them in and I'll do the rest."

We didn't have any luck at first. Two men came sauntering down our lane, but when I spoke to them they glanced up and hurried off. Jarvis was beginning to fume and rustle his lamp shades angrily when a woman came up to the counter and stood there warming herself in my smile. She was a dumpy matron with a contented look, and she poised before me with a birdlike smile. Her head was thrust forward demurely, and her shoulders sagged. I suppose the weight of her breasts must have caused that. She tapered at both ends, like a stretched tear drop, and a black toque was on her head. Bundles were in her arms, and an umbrella jutted out from them.

"Madam," I said, leaning forward, "Sacks greets you and wishes you to be welcome. We are glad you came in. We hope that everyone in your family is well, and that you will spend many happy hours with us. Madam, God bless you and make His light to shine upon you, what is your pleasure?"

The little woman bridled. She put her head on one side and eyed me delightedly.

"How terribly nice!" she said. "What a nice young man . . ."

I shuffled one foot, murmured that it was really nothing, and Jarvis bit me on the ankle. It was quite painful, and I heeled him gently as I leaned forward. The woman was still gazing at me admiringly.

"Now what I want," she said coyly, "is something for Herman, my oldest boy. He's only twelve, you know."

"No!" I answered. "I thought Herman must be all of fifteen by now."

She drew her head back in about fourteen inches and pursed her lips reflectively.

"No." The great breasts heaved sluggishly. "No," she said severely, "Herman could hardly be taken for fifteen." She was trying to be fair to Herman. "Possibly fourteen, or thirteen, but fifteen . . . No, I hardly think so."

"Well," I said, "it's not as though I had counted on it, now is it?" We both simpered moderately at that, and then I took up the attack again. "Madam, you are in luck. Does the boy ever listen to the Purple Yellowjacket on the radio?"

She waggled her head; she wasn't sure.

"Well," I went on, "the most peachy thing you can imagine. Today, not tomorrow or yesterday, the Purple Yellowjacket is in this store, and he has really got something svelte for that scamp of a

Herman."

I stopped and stared down at the dumpy little woman, and she stepped up closer to the counter.

"Oh, fudge," she said. "How stupid of me not to know about the Purple Yellowjacket." She whispered to me, "Who is he?"

I was properly amazed. "Why my admirable woman," I asked incredulously, "do you mean to stand there and tell me that you never heard of that amazing man, that G guy of the sky, that adventurer of the astral orbits called the Purple Yellowjacket?"

She raised the umbrella and would have stayed me, but I rushed on.

"You mean to say you never heard of Brumble's Buttered Crumblies for Little Stumblebums, in the purple and yellow package?"

She was sulking now, and I nudged Jarvis with my foot.

"Well, I'm sure," she said primly, "that Herman knows all about him."

"At twelve?" I shook my head and sneered.

"Yes, at twelve," she answered, "and where is this monstrosity, this Brumble's jacket person?"

I soothed her, "Madam," I said softly, "he is here, and he has one of the brand new Space Hats for Herman. These hats are the result of long years of effort and research by the company's engineers. They are equipped with cross ventilation, pilot light, neon headlights, two-way radio, gyro compass, and a guaranteed death ray. With one of them, Herman can fly like a kite under his own power."

She was staring at me.

"Tush," she said, halfheartedly. "You mean, actually fly?"

My enthusiasm was carrying me away. "Like a damned blue-bottle fly, he can fly," I shouted. "Barrel rolls in the kitchen, loops and spins in the parlor, and power dives in the laundry chute!" I flung out one hand. "Madam, allow me to present the master of the ozone, the Purple Yellowjacket!!"

Jarvis bobbed up beside me. A large scarlet lamp shade was riding on the top of his head, and two smaller conical shades were clamped over his ears. His eyes blazed and his cheeks were puffed. He shot up suddenly and stood there with his staring eyes fixed full on the little woman.

"Alla ma fong!" he moaned, and then crumpled as the woman ripped out a raw quivering scream and slugged him across the head with her umbrella. She hit him and stood there in the center of the aisle, her parcels scattered on the floor, and she was still bawling at the top of her lungs, like a woman having both legs cut off.

The umbrella had torn through the light silk of the shade as nothing, and Jarvis was down on the floor with blood gushing from his scalp. The two small shades were still fitted neatly over his ears, and he did look like a space adventurer, albeit one who had come to considerable grief. In fact, as he lay there with his own blood darkening the wrecked fabric of the large shade that was jammed down across his eyes, he looked as though he might have been mangled between two comets.

People began to rush down the aisle toward us as the woman kept up her screaming, and Bradley and Perry came running back from the hat department to kneel beside the stunned Jarvis. With some difficulty, I got the woman to stop her bellowing, although she was still shaking all over. The crowd was banked around us on all sides, and I looked out over their collective heads.

I could see two blue uniforms start across the store, and I called out the information to Bradley. He and Perry lifted Jarvis up, by the arms. His eyes gradually cleared, and he started to push through the crowd. He was a bit unsteady, and the smaller shades were still on his ears, a fact which enchanted the populace. I was kneeling down, picking up the woman's bundles, and I called out to Jarvis.

"Hey, Cavin, why don't you show the woman how the Space Hat works?"

He must not have heard me. He weaved out of sight, and Fred and Von Perry vanished after him. I tried to hand the woman her packages. She was still breathing heavily, and that great bosom was heaving.

"Madam," I said sorrowfully, "you did something nobody on any of the other worlds could do. You made the Purple Yellowjacket cry." I shook my head mournfully. "This will ruin him with the kids . . ."

She was still watching me like a woman under a spell. She wouldn't take her packages, and she seemed to be paralyzed.

"You shouldn't have done it," I said. "Just wait until Herman hears about it."

And then I went smashing through the crowd to the south doors, and, after leaving the store, doubled around the block to the car.

Jarvis was sitting in the middle of the back seat with a stained handkerchief on his head, and Perry was next to him, howling with laughter. Mumford was sitting in the front seat, and he didn't say anything when I came up, just sat there looking straight ahead. He still had on the dark glasses, and his lean profile didn't turn a fraction of an inch. Bradley started the car, and I got in next to Jarvis. The motor whined and we swung out into traffic.

"It's a terrible thing," I said gravely, panting a little from my dash out of the store. "It's a long, long way to fall. The Purple Yellowjacket, even . . . Jarvis, this will ruin you with the kids."

Perry was wheezing immensely, Bradley hiccoughed with delight, and Mumford's thin chin began to waggle. I could see his shoulders start to shake, and we all went down the street roaring. All, that is, except Jarvis, who seemed depressed.

13

AFTER Mumford's curtailed junket into the business world, we drifted along peacefully for two days. We all needed money to pay our Tonto Club assessments, and so we stayed relatively sober and launched an intensive sales campaign. We heard nothing from Rick and presumed that he was skulking through the mesquite of West Texas, firing his pistol at every gust of wind. We often talked about him, built up long word pictures that inevitably got away from us and grew so astounding that we were forced to abandon them.

My principal recollection of those days is the amazing amount of laughter that filled our lungs and shook us while we lounged around the dirty office. It was almost entirely the mirth of cruelty, and it was so intense that it often became painful and sometimes hysterical. Some one of us would pick up a thread of thought; someone else would establish a ludicrous elaboration of it, and the embellishments would wander far afield, until we were wheezing and choking, laughing at laughter itself. Nothing was outside the province of our bawdy comment, and the state of the state, the citizenry of our town, and the tenets of our faith all came in for an impartial drubbing that usually wound up with Jarvis barking on the couch, Bradley careening around the walls, and Perry and

Mumford snorting madly, eyes wet from hilarity.

It was not all born in bottles. In fact, the major portion of it arose in the unsettling fever of the long times between drinks. We were, I suppose, only young and irreverent iconoclasts whose sole recognizance lay in smashing down, in mirth, the things around us that had incurred our enmity.

It was on one of these somnolent days that Wilfred Garvey came back within our ken. When he sidled into the office, Jarvis was talking on the phone and I was reading the New Yorker. Wilfred was wearing a blue satin polo shirt and whipcord pants were tucked into his gaudy boot-tops. I looked up, nodded my head, and returned to an especially toothsome Arno lady. Jarvis turned around, took the bottle off the desk, and carefully locked it in a drawer.

Wilfred didn't speak. After staring at us for a moment, he went into the bathroom and began shaving. When he had whimpered two or three times, I looked up to see that his hands were shaking so badly that the blade was blurred in passage. Two nicks on his face were streaming blood. I was still watching when Jarvis turned, hung up the phone, and spat on Wilfred's boots. It was a ten or twelve foot carry. I asked Wilfred why he didn't use a lawnmower to shave with, but I wasn't insulting about it. I just asked, and he came charging toward us, waving the razor in parabolas around his head.

"Now, Jimble," he whined, "I can't stand that. Please don't talk like that."

Jarvis was spitting again but he missed this time, because Wilfred jumped all the way across the room from a standing position. Cavin squinted his eyes and smiled.

"Want me to go in the house and get you a towel?" he asked pleasantly.

Wilfred took an involuntary step toward him.

"Say, gee, Cavin," he began, but then he drew up and stopped. His look altered. "What a dirty black-hearted bitchly bastard you are," he said bitterly, and sat down in one of the cane-bottomed chairs.

When he was seated, he began to cry, and his simian face wrinkled like inward drawstrings were tugging at it. He was clutching at the scant hairs on his head, and some of them came out in his clenched fists, so I unlocked the desk drawer and poured him a drink.

He had to make three trys to catch the glass of gin I held out. I may have moved it on him a little bit. His pale eyes watered quickly when the drink scorched at his belly, and he clung to the table for support, his eyes closed. The hair on his conical head was bunched; he looked like a fatigued and antiquated cupid, and he smelled sweaty and beerish.

"You saved my life, Jimble!" he murmured, and then without warning, he capped this climactic utterance by bouncing straight up out of his drooped position. He kicked the chair over and strode out of the office, and Jarvis and I began to laugh, but he only circled the garage and came back in with mincing steps. When he was back in the center of the room, he stopped and wrung his hands.

"Let's go over," he said suddenly, "and frig all the celebrities in Dallas."

I poured another drink and he got it first grab. Jarvis was staring at him.

"Have you got something nice over there, in the way of the deep V, Garvey?"

Wilfred beamed, and passed a trembling hand over his mouth. "Why Jarvis," he said, "they'll take it away from you over there."

"Is that a fact?"

"Damned well betcha. Same way in Shreesport."

I looked at him closely. "You mean Shreveport, Wilfred."

He was humming.

"Sure," he repeated, "down at Shreesport." He considered the ceiling at length. "I used to make three thousand dollars a month down at Shreesport."

This time Jarvis poured him a drink, and we took one ourselves. We were a trifle awed.

"How was that?" I asked.

Wilfred fingered his drink. "Cotton," he said. "Bad month when I didn't make four thousand dollars . . ."

Jarvis looked at me. "Jesus, what a promotion," he whispered. "A thousand dollar raise between drinks."

Mumford came in the door, and Cavin spat at his feet, but missed again. He had one for three. Mumford sat down on the desk swinging his legs, and I turned back to Garvey. I didn't want him to cool off any.

"What about this Dallas situation?"

He rocked back and forth, pleased to be the center of attention.

"Jimble," he confided, "a good lookin' boy like you would have to wear a steel trap in his pants over to Dallas."

It sounded good and Cavin came back in.

"You ever been married, Wilfred?"

Garvey didn't answer for a minute. It seemed to me that a man ought to have information like that at his fingertips.

"Sure," he said sullenly. "I was married once."

Mumford was taking a drink out of the bottle, and his thin face quivered.

"How was it?" he asked, choking, and again Wilfred hesitated before making up his mind.

"I don't know," he muttered finally, between compressed lips, "I didn't never get any of it."

I could understand why he was angry, but Mumford and Jarvis took off in a high, cackling burst of laughter. Jarvis recovered first.

"You're not talking about that orange-headed whore we saw in McKinney when we went up to look at those cattle?"

Wilfred winced. "Don't say that," he cried out. "That girl is as pure as a nun."

Jarvis took a drink.

"She is a whore, and a Jewish whore at that," he said flatly, and Wilfred cavorted around the room, clenching and unclenching his hands.

"She is not a Jew," he screamed. "She never even heard of a Jew. A Jew can't even get into McKinney." He began to cry again and I poured him another drink, but smaller, since the bottle was ebbing. What he said wasn't reasonable.

"Don't you reckon," I asked soothingly, "you might be able to sneak a Jew into McKinney late at night?"

His head rolled in denial, and his voice was thick and deeply pained.

"No! No!" he shouted, "Goddammit, they won't let any kind of Jew in there . . ."

He went weaving over to the couch and dropped on it, crying heavily. It was getting dark, and the rest of us started home for dinner. Outside the door, I told Cavin that Garvey had something on his mind, that he wasn't really that bad. Jarvis stopped dead still and shook his head stubbornly. Then he went back and opened the office door.

"Jew-lover!" he hissed, and even in the gloom, we could see Wilfred jump. When Cavin came back, he went into his house, and I took Mumford home. As we drove through the lengthening shadows, a newsboy shouted that Hitler had made another seizure. But the newsboy's voice was only a shrill small irritation among the other noises that crowded into an urban American twilight.

14

I WAS an Albanian peasant woman when Wilfred walked up the next day. Five of us were at the country club, lounging on the grass around the pool, and I had a heavy towel draped around my head with only a portion of my face jutting out. Buddy Perry was rolling backwards, chortling with glee, and Nancy, his slender blond wife, was smiling indulgently. Cavin was laughing too, and Bradley's face had quivered. Most of them I had going, but the stragglers worried me and I went after them. I rearranged the towel and turned again.

"Albanian peasant woman with wart on nose."

That knocked Perry out again, but he didn't count. Jarvis began to go, and Fred broke into outright smiling. They were all at that moment when you either get them overboard or lose them entirely, and the thing disintegrates. Wilfred came up and stood over me.

"Where's the wart?" he asked, his equine face very serious. The question was irrational and it killed the mood of gentle lunacy.

"Where the hell do you think it is, you Gainsville brush-ape?" I shouted. "I had it removed."

He shifted on his feet. "Then why mention it at all?"

It was over, so I threw the towel away.

"I just mentioned it," I said acidly, "because how else are you going to tell one Albanian peasant woman from another?"

The beer in the glass was cool going down my throat. Around us, on the grass, were quite a number of empty bottles, and the dowagers and matrons clucked disapprovingly as they herded their bright-eyed progeny past us. Wilfred was still standing up, looking around in his alert, birdlike way, and Jarvis twisted over on his stomach and shaded his eyes from the sun.

"Who the hell sent for you?"

Wilfred shifted from foot to foot. "Now, Jarvis . . ." he began.

"Are you a member of this club?" inquired Cavin. "The answer is no, of course not. Now beat it."

Garvey fumed. "Jarvis," he quavered, "a suckin' hog has got more manners than you."

Cavin turned back over and snorted. "A hog," he said crisply, "has got to get along with other hogs like you. I don't." He chewed reflectively on a blade of grass. "Beat it, Wilfred, because you are not only baldheaded, but a business failure."

Wilfred smiled and sat down. He reached into his brush jacket and pulled out three one hundred dollar bills. Then he tossed them out on the grass.

"Need a little coffee money, Jarvis?" he asked, and I realized that he had been waiting nearly thirty minutes to do it. He was sitting with his shoulders thrown back and he nearly lost his money. If Fred and I hadn't collided in midair and thrown Perry off to one side, he would have. Jarvis made his leap, too, but he was farther away and fell short. Wilfred grabbed the money and hastily stuffed it into his pocket, keeping one hand over it.

"Jesus!" he said. "I thought you all came from good families. Jesus!"

He sat there, still guarding his money, and the sunlight beat down on us like a solid covering. Through its yellow glare, Cavin saw the chairman of the greens committee coming down the walk. It was choleric little Busby, the best caddy-curser in the State of Texas. As he came waddling toward the pool, Cavin went across the grass and up the ladder to the diving platform, his tanned legs flashing. Even from the ground, we could see him time the jump.

He waited until the fat little man made the corner, and then he came off the board, got a flip in, and doubled up for his cannonball. When he smacked into the water, a wave plunged up and bent over the side of the pool, striking with geometrical precision; the slanting wall washed out and engulfed Mr. Busby, hitting him and trickling down around him to the ground.

The chubby man was solidly wet, and he began an impassioned peroration that was unfamiliar to most of those listening. Perry was lying on his back and his head was cocked critically.

"If he can hold out another minute," was his considered opinion, "that language will dry him right off."

Almost everyone was laughing, and the collective mirth was not soothing Mr. Busby a great deal. He was standing at the edge of the pool when Cavin broke water.

"Damn your impudent eyes," he shouted, "what'd you splash me for?"

Jarvis was shocked. "Why Br. Busby," he answered, "I had no idea you were there."

Busby waved a dripping fist. "I'll have you suspended from this pool for life," he cried, but Cavin was already out on the bank, ministering to the irate gentleman with continental courtesy, crying for Seth, the life guard, to bring towels, and helping out in a general way. He walked all the way back to the clubhouse with Busby, bending over him and apologizing, and when the damp gentleman had vanished into the locker-room, Cavin turned and came back across the lawn in a dead run, smacking the water in a racing dive. Two strokes brought him to our side of the pool, and he pushed his sleek head over the rim.

"I kind of doused that bastard, didn't I?" he asked gaily, and, throwing up his hands, went sliding back inertly into the water. A torrent of bubbles rushed to the surface.

Wilfred shook his head in deep perplexity. "I can't understand it," he said slowly. "If I tried to get away with the things he does, I'd spend half of every year in jail."

He was brooding over it when I remembered something.

"Yeah," I said. "Sure, Wilfred. But where did you get all that dough?"

He shrugged. "Little cattle deal."

Nancy Perry was drying her hair. "Now, Wilfred," she chided, "you know you haven't been on the stock yards all week, and you were broke yesterday."

She had a nice voice, and her long blond hair cascading down over the yellow bathing suit was disturbing. I turned away, toward Garvey. That is, after awhile I turned away.

"What about it?"

He was looking down at the grass. "I told you straight," he persisted. "I closed a little deal up around home."

Behind him, Perry yawned and stretched.

"You tell a lie now, Willie," he said. "You went out to Fred Burney's Terrace and won that lettuce knuckling them dice." He stopped and yawned more largely, fingering his straw thatch. "Tracey, stick man out there, told me he wouldda won the damned joint if he'da bet his money. Said he was hottern a rock, but pitched his guts. Made fourteen passes once, Tracey said, drawin' down every damned time."

Buddy lapsed into silence, as though the very thought of such chiseling grieved him beyond adequate expression.

"It was fifteen passes," muttered Wilfred abstractedly. "Was a Jew woman from Dallas toted off thirty-seven hundred bucks on my licks. I ought to have got well . . ."

Jarvis had come up and was drying himself off.

"Still hobnobbing with Jews, hunh Garveberg?" he asked, and, as always, Wilfred got unreasonably angry.

"Hell no," he snarled, "I never even looked at her. I can't help it if a Jew woman walks in and rides me."

"Maybe she was a celebrity," suggested Cavin, and Perry gazed at Wilfred admiringly.

"And rode him too!" he said.

Wilfred cried out again. "Nothing like that," he bellowed, and the belief became settled in my mind that the Jews, somewhere, somehow, had used him unkindly. It is a thing they can do.

While we were sitting there drinking the last of the beer, Marsha Locker swept by in a black satin cape with a bathing suit of the same material under it. Absurdly high soled shoes were on her feet, and her pale skin against the satin was startling. Nancy Perry was watching in that detached, scientific way women have when they observe one another, and Cavin raised up and brandished a beer bottle wildly.

"She had better not," said Nancy quietly, "let that sunlight hit her."

Perry stood up and scratched his bare belly with both hands. "Tsk, tsk, my little redhot," he murmured, and pulled Bradley up from the grass. As we walked in to dress, I was telling Wilfred that Burney was not a sentimental man, that no gambler was, and that philanthropy was foreign to his nature. While I talked, I was watching Nancy walk along in front of us.

Garvey snorted. "I know something," he said, "and I am going back out there tonight. If I can get me another two hundred, I'll be in the clear."

While I thought about it, I borrowed ten dollars. After all, he was going back out there. When I had the ten in my hand, I cautioned him again.

"They'll cut you," I said. "If you're hot, they'll heave in the buffed deuce and dead ace. If that don't stop you, the next pair they sleeve out will. If you know too much and call them, they'll beat your ears into a spiral formation, and either way, you'll get wrecked."

But he didn't believe me.

"Wagner took over eight thousand away from him one night last week," he said stubbornly, as if that proved his point. When I reminded him that Wagner had over eight million in the bank, he still couldn't see it.

"They're all the same dice," he insisted.

Bradley was climbing into his pants, and he looked up, irritation on his broad face. "They are the same for awhile, but they get different quicker than hell," he admonished in his husky voice.

But Garvey was obdurate. He was going to win all the money; he was going to get it all together. Every time he opened his mouth, he got richer and richer.

"Oh, let the dumb bastard go," said Perry wearily, and we went to wring our suits out. Nancy was waiting for us, and she had on clinging silk culottes. As we walked toward the car, I was thinking how glad I was that I had a date with Lucille for Tuesday night. As we walked toward the car, I made up my mind to call her when I got home. Just to chat.

15

THE chickens back of the Mirrolite office had always fascinated Bradley. They were peculiar looking fowls of an immense size, and had few tail feathers. When business was slack, Fred used to draw up a chair to the window and sit there for hours, watching. He even had names for all of them, and when we were drinking, his interest became an obsession. He believed they had eagle blood in them, and I suppose he expected to see, one day, an eagle drop down from the sky in a parental, rather than ravenous, role. As the summer weeks slipped by and nothing happened, his enthusiasm began to wane, but he did not forget his feathered flock entirely.

On Monday morning, Jarvis and I came back to the office from town, where we had been paying our dance assessments. As we got out of the car and approached the door, Cavin wrinkled his nose. There was a strange odor about, a pungent smell that assailed the nostrils, and, quickening his step, Cavin rushed in the door ahead of me. I was following fast, and I heard him let out a great shout.

"Bradley," he cried, "what in God's name are you doing?"

I walked in behind him and looked over his shoulder. Fred was naked to the waist, kneeling down over a kettle of steaming water, and in his hands was one of the large chickens, half picked. What we had smelled was the scalded feathers, and I dropped into a chair and started laughing.

"No, I'm not drunk," burst out Bradley, "but you bastards owe me seventeen dollars, and I was hungry."

Jarvis was over by the window, staring out at the chickens.

"Christ Almighty," he said, "you would have to get the best-laying hen out there. Here we have just come back from paying your dance assessment, and you got to do a thing like this. It'll flatten my old lady cold. I oughta call the police."

Bradley went on plucking the huge chicken. Matted yellow feathers were all over the place, and a fire was going in the little iron stove. The room was hot, and I moved my chair into the bathroom just as Cavin went out the door muttering "thief!" under his breath. I asked Fred how came him to kill the chicken.

He was smiling when he looked up; his lightly pitted face glistened from working over the hot water.

"Jimble," he said, "I had one hell of a time with him. Just like runnin' down a damned ostrich." He paused and wiped his broad brow, remembering the glory of the chase. "He'd be in a corner an' I'd tear in after him and bust into the side of the pen. Took me twenty minutes to catch him, and five more to wring his rubber neck." He put his fingers into the breast of the nearly naked chicken. "But my," he finished off admiringly, "ain't he fat?"

He had nearly all of the feathers removed when Jarvis stalked back in, saying nothing. I took off my shirt, and, seizing one great leg, started helping Fred. Cavin got on the couch and sat there cross-legged, watching us.

"Damn your thievin' hide, Bradley," he said, "what'd you do it for? Them are show poultry."

Fred still didn't say anything, just kept plucking, and after a few minutes, Cavin spoke again.

"Bradley," he asked, "are you sure you can cook them things so they are good to eat?"

Bradley said that he had cooked lots of them at military camp, and when he was through talking about his prowess as a cook, Jarvis reached in his pockets and drew out a handful of knives and forks and some salt and pepper shakers. He put them on the table, and I started laughing again. Fred told him we would need a pan and several other things, and he got up. He was halfway out the door when he turned.

"Notice!" he said. "Next time we got to get a smaller one . . ." and then he went after the other things.

The chicken was nearly gone when Wilfred came in the door. We looked up, our faces greasy, and saw that he was in bad shape. Half drunk for one thing, and his queer sartorial elegance was missing entirely. His dark eyes were heavily bloodshot, and his clothes were shabby. When he asked for a piece of chicken, I handed him one, but he only snapped at it a couple of times, and turning around, ran into the bathroom and voided his stomach.

When he came back, his leathery face wasn't clean. I told him to go wash it, and he turned around again. This time he just stuck his head through the doorway and asked me if it was all right. I never saw a man so whipped. He came back in and sat down, and we all watched him. Under our eyes, he tried to whistle. He couldn't do it. He tried to smile at us. It was a failure, and his face sagged back to utter sadness.

"All right." Jarvis said it between bites of chicken.

"What's that, Cavin?"

Jarvis wiped his mouth carefully. "I don't know. That's the reason I asked you. What septic tank did you sneak out of?"

Wilfred looked down at the dirty clothes he was wearing. "Oh, these. . . ."

"Oh . . . yes," said Jarvis. "Those. And that cut-rate face."

Wilfred put his hands up to his face. There was no fight in him; he just sat there with sweat beading out on that high simian forehead of his, and his lips were trembling. He was about to cry.

"How much?" I whispered, and he started.

"What . . . ?" he gibbered. "Ahhh . . . I'm just tired."

I agreed with him. I said that he looked tireder than a blown-out innertube. "But how much did you go for?"

"Nothing." His eyes kept flickering around ceaselessly, like those of a cornered animal. "None of that stuff."

"You are a particularly stupid liar," I said. "How much was it?"

He shook his head and gave up.

"Five hundred," he whispered, so low that we could hardly hear him. Then he put his head down in his hands and started shaking. He wasn't crying, just shaking like a man naked in the cold.

"He said he lost five hunnert," hummed Bradley. "That means he went for anyway a grand. Whoee!"

Even Cavin was silent, and the three of us sat there and watched him shiver in the hot room. He was like a lean dog throwing off water, and the quivers hit him in spurts. He would be immobile, and then he would start shaking.

"I got to have a drink," he burbled, without looking up. We didn't have anything but a pint of the gin, and he downed a glass of that in one drink. He heaved it at his mouth like a man watering a lawn, and we watched him with a detached, scientific interest.

"If he holds that shot," murmured Jarvis, "he'll either be drunk or dead."

He held it, and gradually his heaving abated. In less than a minute he had another drink and began to take hold of himself. The tremor went out of his voice and he toned up generally, began to talk with an air of drunken bravado.

"Men," he said, "I got hooked just like you thought I was going to. I was nine hunnert winner once, but I guess they rung the killers in on me, because the next thing I knew, I was three hunnert waster and on the skids. After I started down, I couldn't hold wind or water. Lost three hunnert and seventy-five cash, five hunnert on one check, and four hunnert and eighty-five on another one."

What he was doing to himself was a form of masochism, and Jarvis called out sharply.

"Give me those figures again," he said.

Wilfred smiled benignly. "Yep," he went on, "over thirteen hunnert." He took another nip at the bottle. "Besides the Jewish woman, I was the biggest shooter out there."

We all stared at him.

"Yes, indeed," I said, "you must be quite a big-time Charles. How long before you hit the skids did Burney drop by the table?"

He meditated. The gin had oiled his eyes. "Oh, he come up back of me when I was so hot. I bet I had him worried."

Fred grunted softly. "Yeah, I bet he was scared to death," he put in, and Cavin looked at Wilfred with wondering eyes. He raised both hands in the prayer attitude.

"Peace," he said solemnly, "peace, because it is wonderful beyond compare."

Wilfred was smiling at his boots, basking in the adulation, and I mixed a gin and water drink.

"Garvey," I said, holding the glass up, "here's to you, the most remarkable man I know. In fact, the only man I ever knew who woke up in a brand new world every morning."

"Oh, shoot," said Wilfred. "I didn't hardly sleep at all last night, as a matter of fact."

He was smiling wanly, fretting over his insomnia, when he bolted suddenly from his chair and began to circle the room, pounding the sides of his head and moaning.

"Bless Patty," he cried out on the third time around, "that biggest one was a packing company check."

Fred thrust out his big head incredulously. "You mean it was on the company? It was for cattle?"

When Wilfred paused to nod his head mutely, we looked at each other. Jarvis whistled softly and shook his head in disbelief.

"Maximum of twenty years," I intoned, "minimum of two."

"Gawdalmighty!" Fred whispered, "embezzlement."

Wilfred was crying. The tears were streaking his dirty face and silvering the stubble on his chin. "I just took it out there for flash," he lamented. "I didn't think he'd get it away from me."

"The other check," I asked, "was that personal?"

He was nodding at me when the phone rang. We all jumped at its clamor. Jarvis took it off the hook and said "yes?" Then he listened for a few minutes, and hung the instrument back up with the flourish of one having news.

"That was Perry," he said, turning to us. "Burney just sent two men by the house. Said they wanted to see you at the Continental National Bank tomorrow at two o'clock. Told Perry it would be a good idea for you to be there."

It was beginning to get dark, and the fire in the little stove had burned low. We all watched Wilfred. He started to sit down, and halfway, changed his mind and got back up again. He was solidly drunk and he floundered about the room, mouthing about how his old man would get him out of it. He had the look, in the darkening room, of a mired animal.

"I got to get to McKinney," he wailed.

Nobody said anything, and Jarvis got up with a jerk and walked to the window. He was turned away from us when he spoke.

"I've got no sympathy for the bastard. We warned him." He turned around. "You're a bald-headed business failure, Garvey, and you are all through . . ." Jarvis was excited, his voice was tingling in the dusky room, and when Wilfred had dejectedly drained the last of the gin, Cavin kept after him, worried him, and snarled at him. "You can't go, Wilfred. You never were anything but a dunce, and now you are a bigger dunce. You are a common thief and an embezzler. You are all washed up, and the soap has been thrown away. To hell with you . . ."

Garvey looked at us, his mouth sagging and wet lanes down his cheeks. Jarvis finally quit talking and it grew quiet. A train went chuffing through the valley below and trailed up a plume of black smoke that feathered away and disappeared into the grey sky. In the stillness, Bradley spat on the stove, and there was a soft hiss. As we watched, all silent shapes around the room, Wilfred staggered over to the couch, fell on it like a silhouette of despair, and threw up his hands.

"A business man," he sobbed, "trapped by high school boys."

The passion of Gethsemane was in his broken voice, and we sat listening to his terrible crying until, in the middle of it, he fell asleep and started snoring gently.

"What'll he do?" asked Bradley.

"His old man will bail him out," answered Jarvis, and moved

toward the door. He flipped the switch and the sudden flare of light stung our eyes, so that we rubbed them hard. Cavin gathered up the silverware and utensils he had brought out from the house, and as we turned to go the only sound was Wilfred's rhythmical snoring.

16

THAT night we got up a pot and collected enough money to send Wilfred home. He left early the next day, on the bus, and he listened to our last minute instructions with great care. His hands were shaking badly and he must have felt like hell. He certainly looked it. The last we saw of him, he was leaning far out of a back window of the bus, waving to us.

When he had vanished into traffic, Jarvis and I got in the car and drove away. It was a little bit after seven o'clock in the morning.

"What are you going to do?" yawned Cavin. "Let's go out to the club and play a round, shall we?" He yawned again, but I was not misled. I only snorted. For one thing, I knew he would get some bets going and chisel me out of several dollars. It was really the only reason he wanted to play golf.

"I think I'll sleep," I said.

People were coming to work. As we passed through the streets we speculated as to how much they made and where they worked, but it was too hard. In that harsh morning light, all the faces seemed bleak and they all looked like clerks to me. The important people were still asleep. We gave it up after a few blocks, and Jarvis dozed off. The collar of a tan polo coat was up around his handsome head, and the too regular lines of his chin and brow were serene against the seat. When we got to his house, I plunged into the driveway and the jolt woke him up.

"How are we going tonight?" he asked sleepily.

What he really wanted to know was, were we going in my car. I told him I didn't know, to call me in the afternoon, and he trudged over the wide lawn and into his house, combing the dark hair as he went. He was only going upstairs to bed, but I suppose he was afraid he might meet someone on the way up. I backed out of the driveway and went home to my own bed.

At nine o'clock that night, I picked him up again and we drove to Ballinger Street Drug Store. The lot was packed with cars, and young gentlemen were parading from car to car, taking drinks from trays hung on the cars and fingering their black or white ties constantly. They did not wear dress clothes often enough to be fully comfortable in them, and their twitching shoulders and fumblings after vests were indications of it. We pulled up in their midst, and Jarvis cursed a few close friends cordially. Over in the corner of the lot, a small group was singing "The Eyes of Texas," and in dim recesses of the parked cars, the white shoulders of the ladies were visible. Their high young voices rippled appreciatively as the boys postured before them.

I suppose every town in the South has a counterpart of Ballinger Street Drug Store, a place where the sons and daughters of the burghers and bankers come to be initiated into the local revels. In appearance, it was not a prepossessing place, only a small drug store on a corner, with a parking lot next to it. The proprietors were stupid men blessed with false heartiness and entirely lacking in any consideration for their trade. The service was atrocious; the place itself staffed by amiable morons. The interior twinkled with everything from plumbing parts to children's toys, and crowded far into the back there could be seen a few small shelves of drugs. However the liquor business was brisk, especially out of the small pool hall next door, which was run by a pleasant brigand called Tony. The tables in this hall were few and the smell septic. What the allure was I cannot say, but for twenty years the younger set of each generation had wended to the spot before its parties, parking and proceeding to instill a glow for greater merriment in the pit of the stomach.

We sat there with the rest of them and were talking and answering greetings when Tommy Estes, a lethargic newspaper photographer, walked over and sat down in the back seat. He was fingering his collar.

"Have a seat," said Jarvis.

Estes leaned up and grinned. He knew Cavin of old.

"I've got to go out," he said, "and take . . . a few pictures . . . of the idle rich cavorting." He talked so slowly that the very process of forming speech seemed to hurt him. "But . . . I guess a pint . . . one pint . . . of whiskey . . . wouldn't hurt anybody."

Jarvis turned half around. "You going to take a picture of me?" he enquired.

Estes considered taking a picture of him.

"No," he said finally, "I guess . . . not. It would be . . . a good picture . . . but it would probably hurt our circulation . . . too much." He trailed his sentences off, as though he weren't sure he had finished.

Jarvis sniffed and I honked the horn and ordered a pint of Canadian Club. When the tray was delivered, we split the check three ways. Estes decided to be an aristocrat, and called for many ingredients with which to mix a drink. It was a mistake, and we sat there talking, Jarvis and I drinking straight. The ratio involved gave us a marked advantage. While we were talking, Mumford came by, his thin face rosy and eager under the glow of the neon sign on the corner. He was well scrubbed and groomed, and his tuxedo fitted nicely, but that fox terrier air was inescapable.

"Hoddy, hoddy, hoddy," he cried, leaning in the window. "Got a very good thing tonight. Very classy, indeed."

"Bring her over," said Jarvis, "and we'll throw a quick lay in her."

Mumford was pained. "This one is straight as a die," he answered reproachfully, and added that he would bring her over. I said that would be fine, and he went away with a flourish. We had a few more, and he came back to the car with a very small girl, handed her into the back seat, and moved in beside her.

"Miss Pollack," he said proudly, "Mr. Jarvis, Mr. Estes, Mr. Jimble."

We chorused softly and I turned the dome light on. Jarvis looked around at her.

"One hundred and four pounds," he murmured. I thought he was long, and I countered.

"Throw back your coat, please," I asked. She looked up at Mumford, a little bit startled. He smiled at her and she opened her wrap. "Not over a hundred," I calculated, "even with a brassiere on."

Her eyes were big and questioning. She had an oval, piquant face.

"Dollar," Jarvis said.

"Bet," I answered, and we all looked at her.

She was being carried a trifle fast. Mumford asked her how much she weighed.

"Ninety-seven. But I gained two pounds last week."

She lifted her chin defiantly, as though she were trying to justify her tininess. I took the dollar from Cavin and put it in my pocket. About that time Estes asked for another drink. Jarvis held up the empty bottle, and Estes was profoundly shocked.

"Why, I ain't had but one drink . . . out of that bottle," he said slowly, and began a moan of protest.

Jarvis said "cry, you bastard, weep," and smiled pleasantly. He was genuinely pleased. Miss Pollack was looking around the car from one of us to the others. Her mouth was vivid and the dress she wore was cut too low for her age. I was watching her when Cavin picked up the straight drink he had been hoarding and asked me for a chaser. In his lamenting, Estes had put the glass containing the remnants of his mixed drink on the tray, and I handed the glass to Jarvis. I had also thoughtlessly flipped ashes in the glass. Jarvis took the neat drink and gulped at the chaser. He almost downed it, but midway in the operation, spluttering seized him.

"Jimble," he choked, "the chaser!"

I handed him a glass of water and he drained it hurriedly, peering at me over the rim of the glass.

Mumford got out, disappointed at not finding a drink, and left us for fairer fields. We said goodbye to Miss Pollack, and she went across the parking lot with Mumford. I believe she was relieved.

"What I want most in life," mused Jarvis, twirling his key chain, "is an acre of breasts like hers to walk on barefooted . . . a solid, tiptilted acre of soft breathing lungs like hers . . ." He trailed off and grunted, as though the very thought of it had stricken him mute.

"Be good," admitted Estes from the back seat, "but I'd like . . . to inhale one . . . down to about here . . ." He motioned at the bottom of his throat, "and then slowly . . . gag to death . . . on it . . ."

It seemed to me they were too enthusiastic about it.

"Oh, I don't know," I said, "I've seen some you could find old newspapers under. Broken bottles, moths, anything . . ."

They obliged me by being silent for a minute, in consideration of the unknown treasure trove beneath certain breasts, and when I roused them by suggesting that we buy another pint of whiskey, Estes came out of his revery.

"I'll be damned," he cried wrathfully. "I'll get my own this time."

We ordered two more bottles, and when we had taken another

drink, Tommy got his camera case and we went out to get Lucille. The lights were brighter as we drove along and sound impinged on the ear with more clarity. Something in the back of my head whispered caution, and I drove the car with extreme care.

The thought was in my mind, as I got out of the car and walked across the lawn, that of all the times I had walked toward houses with girls in them waiting for me, this time and this girl meant a new thing, a thing more earnest. I tried to dissemble the thought of her, to remember her thin shoulders and firm young breasts, her oval face with the grey eyes spaced in it, and the hanging whorls of dark hair. The thrust of her thighs inside a skirt when she walked along was a maggot of thought twisting in a warm part of my mind, and I recalled her air of almost childish solemnity. I could not deny that I had wanted to leave her that night in the hotel, but neither could I deny that I had longed for the touch of her ever since, the smoothness of her shocking my hands.

Her father, a wrinkled, kindly man, was slumped down reading a newspaper when I came into the living room. His eyes were unfathomable behind his glasses, but he was pleasant of greeting.

"Sit down," he said. "Another party?"

It was an attempt at politeness. He knew it was another party, but I smoothed my hair back with one hand and answered that it was another party. We talked shortly about Huey Long's assassination, the chances negro fighter Louis would have with the German Schmeling, and that was all. I sat and watched the lights glinting off the tips of my shoes. I wondered if he could smell the whiskey on me, and my hands shook when I lighted a cigarette. That was a sign I needed two or three more drinks, but I couldn't tell about him. He had retreated halfway behind the newspaper, and I didn't say anything else because I didn't feel that our immediate purposes in life were at all mutual.

The radio at his elbow crackled with a commercial announcement, and we were both listening to an exhortation about toothpaste when Lucille came down the stairs. She came down slowly, as sure of herself as only eighteen can be, and she seemed slender and very virginal in wine colored taffeta. She crossed the room on incredibly high heels and began to rummage in a purse on the mantel, transferring its contents to the smaller one she carried. Both her father and I were watching silently, and when she was through, her dark head went down toward his and her laughter fell across his upturned face. From where I sat, with the whiskey beginning to put pincers of warmth in my belly, the lamp light turned his glasses silver. It made him look blind, a little man looking up at a young girl, a man with silver discs for eyes and a proud smile on his face.

When she turned to me, wariness was in her manner, but I had expected that.

"Shall we go?" she asked, impersonally, and I nodded and heaved up from the cool leather chair. I said good-night to her father and we passed out the door, but as I pulled it shut behind me, I could feel that strange proud smile of his drilling into my back, and see the pale color of his pate under the thinning hair. Lucille's dress whispered softly as we walked toward the car, and I could sense the stubborn temper of her mind. But at the same time, I could see the lift of her breasts under the tight bodice, and their conformity was a vague unrest that had memory for an asset.

It is not the same thing, I told myself; it is a far different thing, but how, exactly, I did not know. I opened the door for her and when she was in, I went around to get under the wheel. Lucille knew Tommy and she spoke to him and nodded to Cavin.

"You have on your three best things," I said lightly, as the car pulled away from the curb.

"And why not?" she asked, smiling at me.

"And why not indeed . . ." I answered, and as I patted her on the knee, I was grieved to discover that she was wearing a garter belt. They are, taken all in all, very irritating garments and I once lost a thumbnail in one, but as I smiled down into her face I knew that the situation was not above handling.

The gravelled court of the club was packed with cars when we arrived, and still more of them were stretched out in rows along the polo field. As we parked and got out, the music was a faint and swinging invitation. Jarvis cut a buck-and-wing on the grass, clicking his heels in conclusion, and we went surging up the stairs of the club. A trumpet was threading around aimlessly above the solidity of the brass section, and as we checked our hats and Lucille's wrap we could hear the steady sliding whisper of dancing feet. Jarvis was jubilant.

"This is the night," he said, rubbing his hands together, "this is the night of nights," and we walked through the crowd to the edge of the dance floor, where Estes unlimbered his camera and began to circle the room. Lucille and I began to dance.

The panelled hall was decked with silver crepe paper and Japanese lanterns flooded down a red radiance from the low ceiling. The orchestra sat in an alcove on the far side of the floor, and the napery of the long wall tables was blushed under the lanterns. White shoulders welded to russet coats wheeled up and down the hall, and a curious sibilance floated over the throng. Gradually, as you watched, the white shoulders came to have faces, and their escorts came to be entities, with different ways of smiling or holding the head. They were all like parts of a passing show, and I moved about among them with Lucille in my arms.

The tall man with the hesitant drag in his right leg was Whittlesy, an insurance agent who could drive a golf ball out of sight. His partner, very small below his shoulder, was Mrs. Collins, the wife of the local Buick dealer, and I wondered how much of a Buick had gone to buy the gown she wore, because its simplicity was a tribute to its cost. Banker Lightner came by, grave and pompous even to music, and he was holding Mrs. Pemberton, our best grocer's wife, a dimpled, dumpy little woman who was earnestly trailing her breasts around the room but never quite caught up with them. Dorothy Bird, an antiquated debutante, swept by with a toothy lad some years her junior, but I was glad to see that Dorothy was still trying. When she had flourished into the pack, I turned to see Broderick Warstler go swinging by with Marsha Locker. Marsha had on a dark clinging dress, and her lissome body flowed along very close to the big man's hip. Behind him, and in rude contrast, stout Alfred Jeffers reduced the dance to a mild form of athletics with his large wife. I was watching him stumble along when Harold, Lucille's fiance, tagged me. I gave her up after making a ceremony of shaking hands with him and praising his general appearance.

They danced off, he talking very earnestly about something, and I lighted a cigarette. Standing there, I caught a glimpse of Cavin whirling with Lorraine Johnson, who had passed through three husbands and seemed fit for three more. Her head was thrown back, her wide mouth was laughing, and Cavin's dark head was close to hers. Then they too were sucked back into the maelstrom of the music, and all the shoulders turned and the feet whispered along.

They were all there. As far back as I could remember, they were all there. True, some of them had their heads down, plowing painfully, and others swept along with a practiced ease, but it was a remarkable commentary that those who passed with an elfin grace had by far the least money. An axiom was involved, but I didn't stop to work it out because I saw Lucille pass, and as the music stopped, I took her out of her fiance's arms. It didn't please him very much. In fact, he looked as if he might be having stomach pains, but I took her anyway.

The wine colored taffeta flowed away from her shoulders, moulded her hips, and flared largely at the bottom. We didn't say a word until the music began again, and then I gathered her close. Not too close, not a seizure and search of her body, but close enough that the movements of her breasts and thighs were lightly against me.

"It is not logical, having known greater joys, that I should be stirred by dancing with you," I said, and she lifted the hand that was on my shoulder and slapped me lightly.

"If you don't shut up," she whispered, "I'll never forgive you. Both Harold's mother and father are here tonight."

The whiskey had mantled to my head with a pleasant glow.

"If that is what you want," I said, very close to her ear, "if you want to marry child Harold and lie awake next to him at night and hear him snore, and join the Junior League and confuse poor families with gifts and have children and develop that middleaged spread and grow old gracefully delivering papers on the state of culture in the Balkans while the ladies crouch in pigeontoed wonder and drink in your wisdom, if you want to hold cozy little teas and agonize when somebody drops a cup and mismatches your set . . . if you want to live in a house on the fifth green and play at being business man's solace when he lugs his passion home from the filing cases . . ."

She put her hand over my mouth and we went along through the music with that strong feeling of oneness. It was a moment when friction was released, and we wheeled lightly through an enchanted void of sound. After the music stopped, I lighted a cigarette and blew smoke in her face. She didn't flinch.

"Remember the plumber and his wife?" I asked.

She said she remembered, and while we were smiling at each

other, Harold came up back of us and froze to a full point. When the music started, he bolted forward and I pressed her hand in leaving. It was just one of the little niceties every woman should receive. While I was standing there, watching her pivot away, I decided to go down to the bar and talk to Bradley. There was no question of whether or not he would be there.

He was there, but Mr. Barney was standing beside him, so I postponed my arrival. Back in the locker room, a bunch of dead game sports were flipping the dice, and the green top of the pool table looked like a lettuce patch. Cavin had the dice as I walked up. He cast them, and two spots turned up on each die. He then bet ten dollars that he would make the four, and the gentlemen dived for his money like kingfishers, but he came out third roll three and one. As I walked away, I could hear the bitter lamentations of the losers and I agreed with them, but it was a knack Cavin had, that business of throwing fours. It was an ability that had cost me, through the years, the equivalent of a good sized apartment house.

The bar was packed and smoky. Bradley was sitting alone, rotating a jigger glass in his fingers, and his broad face was impassive. He brightened when I came up, however, and took a quick drink out of the bottle. When it was down, he wiped his mouth and gazed at me apologetically.

"I hate to do that," he said, "and I know it looks like hell, but I am a prohibition boy. These people are so goddamned polite I get nervous and frantic . . ."

Looking around, I agreed with him. They were sitting at round wooden tables, and their smiles were either set in politeness or loosened by drink. I told Fred that Jarvis was gutting the crap game, and we were about to have a drink on the handsome one's luck when Mr. Brandley, a lawyer, came over from one of the tables and shook hands with me. I introduced him to Fred, and both of them bowed with great elegance. Mr. Brandley was pleasantly gone.

"Knew your father," he said, turning to me and wagging his head sagely. "We're expecting great things from you, m'boy."

I didn't know just what we were expecting, but I murmured that I hoped I wouldn't be a disappointment. Mr. Brandley had climbed up in my face, almost, and he was beaming paternally.

"Nonsense!" he shouted, clapping me on the shoulder. "Y'r old Dutch's boy. You've got the Stuff."

I appreciated having the Stuff, and involuntarily I thought of Lucille. Before me, Mr. Brandley's face was twisting; he was chewing out his words, bidding me be diligent, telling me there was always room at the top. He started away, after shaking hands again, but halfway across the room he stopped and turned for a final word.

"Don't ever f'rget it," he bellowed across the heads of those sitting at the tables, "y'r father had it an' you've got it . . . got that old Stuff."

He punched mightily at the smoky air, smiled vaguely, and sat down. I was aware of the brief regard of the whole room. For one second I was the focal point of their eyes. I guess they wanted to see a man who had the Stuff.

Fred held out his glass. "Maybe if I had another drink," he said, "there'd be room at the top for me too."

We were sitting there, seeing if we couldn't find room at the top for Fred, when Mumford came in with the ninety-seven pounder. She had been drinking and her eyes were bright with it. Just as I was beginning a lecture on the evils of drink, Mumford poured her a drink of our whiskey. It was discouraging, in a way.

She took the drink hard, but it went down, and Mumford had one for himself. Then he winked at me; he was trying to palm the diminutive lady off, and it didn't look that tough so I led her upstairs, explaining that the clubhouse had been part of a British fort during the Revolutionary War. She said that seemed like a long way from the fighting, but I explained that these troops had overshot the Ohio Valley and had been too tired to get back.

There is something about dancing with small feminine persons that is entirely soothing to the male ego. The protective urge bursts out in full flower, and, inescapably, we look for dragons on the edge of the dance floor. As I took Miss Pollack along with me through the lilting strains of the music, I was aware of her finely formed body. This last is a thing I always mention in connection with my dancing partners, but there is no way to avoid it. It is a thing I always notice, and I bemoan the day when I shall not.

"Like the party?" I asked, and she said she liked it very much. Someone bumped us and we started out at another angle. "I like your gown," I said, and she smiled up at me.

There was an interesting shadow in the valley between her breasts, and I wasn't lying or being polite. I did like her dress. When the music stopped, I suggested that we stroll around the pool and look at the Indian graves.

"Indians?" Her eyes were wide.

"Only dead ones," I replied, "and I will protect you."

On the way to the doors we passed Lucille and I bowed deeply. I nearly didn't get back up again, and then Miss Pollack and I went down the stairs hand in hand. It delighted me to know that Lucille was staring after us.

Miss Pollack never did get to see the Indian graves, but after two turns around the pool and one around the polo grounds, I was forced to revise my original opinion of her age by at least two years. Finally, she said she had to go back in, and I scoured my mouth with a handkerchief.

"But about this late date you promised me . . ." I said.

The moon was half strangled by a scud of clouds and the air was balmy. I was trembling a very little bit, as I always do when on fresh spoor. She stood in front of me, her hands in mine, and I rubbed my cheek against hers. She said that she never gave late dates, but that her address was 607 Riverview Drive and to wait at the side. I promised her that I too was opposed to such dates, and that I would be there at three o'clock. Then I took her back to the club and when the Hot Horse cut in, I thanked her and went back to the bar.

Fred was leading a group in South Sea Island Magic, and the din was terrific. It finally drove me back to the locker room, where I took a shower. The intent ring of faces was still hung over the crap table, and as I was putting my stiff shirt back on, Jarvis came walking toward me with a double handful of crumpled bills. He held them in front of my face until I nodded, and then we went out to the car for a fresh bottle, one to use in celebrating his good luck.

The gravel of the driveway whispered harshly beneath our shoes. The country club was a bulking rectangle of lights at our back, and the music was an insistent beat that made the whole night pound. Jarvis went along badly. My own head was heated, but from the corner of my eye I could see his legs moving oddly and stiffly, like he only put them out to keep from falling down. In our passage down between the lanes of parked cars, we went by a figure vomiting. His back was to us; he was half draped over a fender, and we could see his shoulders jerking.

When we got to the car, I fumbled the key out of my vest pocket and unlocked the door. Jarvis was behind me, swaying and popping his knuckles impatiently, and when I brought the bottle out he reached for it.

"Jimble," he said heavily, "this is the extra drink, the one that makes the big difference."

I didn't say anything, and he took the extra, big difference drink. From the size of it, I could see how it might make a difference. When the bottle came down, his face was a twisted mask. Under the moonlight, it was the face of an anguished gargoyle.

Far to the right, a car pulled out of line and began to growl across the polo field. It came toward us with a mounting whine, two increasing spots of light, and then it charged into the rail board of the field and went roaring down the seventeenth fairway. Back of us, the music stopped with a faint flourish of brass, and we sat down on the running board. I had a short drink, and when it had trailed that bitter warmth down my throat, I coughed and spat on the grass.

"No good," said Jarvis thickly.

"No?"

"No." He waved an inclusive hand at the country club. "Try to lov'm but can't. Nothing there. Pack 'a fools."

"Jus' so. Win lots money tonight. Have terrible head t'morrow, but's truth."

"Ah." It wasn't much to say, but I said it as sagely as I could, and a girl laughed suddenly, in one of the cars near us. It was a forced sound, and Cavin's head came up. He stared fixedly in the general direction of the sound.

"Bitch!" he shouted, but there was no answer. He kept staring fiercely into the shadows, and the bottle came to my mouth again. The smell of it sickened me, but I took two swallows and fought nausea, felt it wear away.

"You drinkin' too much," said Jarvis. After it was safe for me to speak, I said I guessed I was, and he had one, staring at me reprovingly. Then he got up and began to talk, pounding on the fender for emphasis. From what I could gather, he thought we were all hollow people, and that while we might have guts enough to take dope, we didn't have enough guts to take a lethal dose. The whole content of his speech was morbid. I kept nodding and he kept talking, in an angry, slurred voice, and then Buddy Perry came walking out of the shadows with a girl wearing a rhinestone dress. She was a tall girl and made a tapestry of sparkles as she came toward us.

"I figured it would be this way," said Perry. "I knew it." He was quite jocular. The girl stopped short of the car and I couldn't see her face. "Man alive," crowed Perry, coming forward, "this is a pussy-cat of a party, ain't it?"

He took the bottle out of my hand and drank from it. The girl hesitated.

"Quite all right," I said, "come in the house."

She gave a small embarrassed laugh, and I knew I wasn't interested in her. Sure enough, she was wearing an ordinary face, and she needed every one of the rhinestones. She was large in the breast, however, so I could understand Perry's interest, as he has a gross streak.

Perry was about to introduce her, but Jarvis said that it wouldn't be necessary, that he already knew more people than he could handle, and we all had a drink in tight silence. As we walked back toward the club house, the music stopped and we could see the dancers begin crowding down the stairs.

The ball was over, and after I found Lucille, got her wrap, took a drink, and found Jarvis again, we drove downtown to the Blackstone coffee shop and ate. Lucille was enormously polite to me, and wouldn't even give me a kiss when I took her home. I kissed her anyway, and her nails sliced into my cheek neatly. She stood there in the dark doorway, tense and near tears, and I bowed my head artfully, so that the blood dripped down onto my shirt-front. When she turned and went inside, I walked back across the lawn to the car, smiling to myself.

17

JARVIS and I were driving back from her house when the piercing wail started up. It was a thin screaming sound, and I eased off on the foot-feed and listened. It was an ambulance, and when it came careening down West Seventh Street, we pulled out after it. It went by us like a white blur, but we gathered speed and began to gain. The night wind was searching, and it played like frozen breath at the back of my head, which was still a trifle moist from the shower I had taken. When the ambulance pulled up, we parked behind it and jumped out.

Cars lined each side of the road and their headlights flung out brilliance, stabbing lanes of light that people were hurrying through. The wrecked car was on its side, and in the glare of the headlights it looked like a smashed black bug. One wall was caved in, and the motor was in the front seat. It was a well-wrecked car, and the index to its condition was readable and simple. The road had turned but the car had not.

Three men were tugging at something through a partially opened door, and one of them cursed as his hat fell off. His voice was flat and vindictive in the night. Behind him, the white-coated ambulance men brought up a stretcher, but the men around the car were having trouble. Their muffled instructions floated over to us, and when they attempted to right the car, Jarvis and I stepped forward and helped, but it wouldn't turn. Then the barehead man got a crank and smashed away at the windows, a task rendered difficult by the starred and shattered safety glass. After a few more minutes of breaking out the pin-pointed knives of glass, two of them lifted the driver out.

It was a limp body and small, in dress clothes. A gusty sigh went up from the onlookers, and as the stretcher men came toward me, I stepped back. The body was twisted a little, knees drawn up and shoulders flat, and half of the face belonged to Mumford. I didn't recognize the other half. The blood that dripped from that alien half stained the stretcher black under yellow starlight.

"Mother 'a God," breathed Jarvis behind me, "it's the Hot Horse!" His tone was amazement, but it seemed to me his tense was wrong.

"Cavin," I said, "it was the Hot Horse."

We couldn't get it. We had seen him, but the impact was slow in arriving. It just didn't make any sense that Hot Horse Mumford was blotted out like that. While we were standing there, wrestling with the enormity of it, they brought her by. She looked very tiny under the sheet, and one small white hand dangled over the edge of the stretcher, dangled and swayed with every motion. When the ambulance started back toward town, its whine lifted up with startling clarity, and the crowd, having seen the meat taken out of the grinder, got in its cars and drove away, until only Cavin and I were left there beside the wrecked car. Back of us, the lights of the town sprinkled over the prairie shoulder in a long semicircle, and a speeding car slewed around the corner, slowed down briefly and accelerated again. It was cold.

"Maybe," said Jarvis, "'ey weren't dead . . .," but his voice was thick and unconvinced, and the wind whipped it away. The crumpled car was in front of us, and I remembered vitality and desire flowing through the little girl's lips as they moved against mine, and the touch of her firm breasts. That nerve in my cheek rebelled suddenly, and my mouth was dry. Jarvis was looking at the car.

"Hell of a way to get cold," he whispered, and we turned to go.

"I hope they have boat races in heaven," I told Jarvis as we walked along the side of the dark road. "Mumford sure loved to get a long one home."

It was a stupid thing to say, but it was my way of deferring to death come so suddenly, and we got in the car and drove back to town.

The next afternoon Bradley and Perry came into the Mirrolite office about two o'clock. They looked sober and well-scrubbed, as all pall-bearers should. Cavin and I were to have served in that capacity, but I don't go to funerals. I realize that I shall have to go to at least one, but that appointment is beyond my control. Cavin made no explanation; he just didn't go. Sunlight slanted in through the windows of the office and fell across the littered floor. Bradley was shining his shoes on the edge of the tub, and his voice was distant and wondering.

"Damned if it ain't gettin' dangerous to be a member of this club. There's Rick took a powder, Garvey turned crook, and Mumford gone dead on us."

"Something we drank," I said, and Jarvis looked up from some gold cuff-links he was trying to repair.

"No," he said slowly, "no, it's not that. If you figure to go out hot, like Mumford, you just go, that's all . . ."

"Praise Gawd!" barked Perry. "It didn't take a minute. It is too true. Gawd's name be praised!"

Jarvis didn't like that; his handsome face twisted. "Why, you bullet-headed moron," he said crisply, "you will be infesting the earth when all us good men are gone."

Perry was sucking his orange tooth. "Don't make a damn about me. Maybe I'm smooth as a baby's butt, maybe I'm not. Maybe I'll find mine tomorrow, but the fact remains . . . that won't be the Hot Horse in that coffin." His narrow brow was wrinkled and absorbed in the sunlight. "Won't be any laughter in that box, just a white slug in a pressed suit. We'll pray over it, an' I guess some will cry, but Mumford won't be there. We'll just be satisfyin' ourselves that we done right by him."

Fred came to stand in the door. He was tightening the knot in his dark tie abstractedly, and his bumpy face was puzzled.

"Well," he mused, "the guy wasn't worth much. He was a phony and a louse, but he loved life so much that it don't seem right to have him gone. Remember how he used to walk along so fast, and how he used to kill himself over jokes?"

Bradley was trying to say something he couldn't ever say, and the knowledge of his failure perplexed him. He was trying to talk Mumford back into the room.

"Yeah, I remember," yawned Perry, "but it's just a memory. Let's go." He stood up, stretching his arms. "We'll be back as soon as we put the Hot Horse to bed."

He and Bradley went out the door, and we listened to their footsteps fading down the walk. A beetle buzzed ineffectually at the window, and the drone of his wings fell heavily in the stillness. Cavin had on a silk sport shirt; he was sitting on the cot with his knees drawn up.

"I don't care," he said suddenly, his dark head turned down toward the floor. I told him he was lying, and he began to chew on his knuckles. "Oh, hellfire," he went on, "I'm sorry Mumford went out, but that's not what I mean. Why stay? We are the vanguard of the future; we are the last best hope of earth . . ." He stopped and laughed, but it was unpleasant laughter. "We are the inheritors . . . and we don't even like ourselves . . ."

Motes danced through the fan of sunlight at the window, and a calf bawled down in the valley. It was a large order, but I took a stab at it.

"We've got to want something, Cavin, to want some thing or somebody. And what we want must be important to us, even if it's only a hat or a woman's love or a certain postage stamp. But most of all, we must want people and lights and laughter, because the emptiness must be infinite out there among the stars, out there where Mumford is. Even when the unbeauty of the world stinks in our noses, we must remember what we want . . ." I wasn't getting it; it wouldn't come. "Oh, hell, I don't know for sure, but it's my idea that the butchers have got to want to be good butchers, and the plumbers have to do their best plumbing. It boils down to a kind of stubbornness, an endless insistence against the ill winds . . ."

"Burmashave," said Jarvis quietly.

It didn't bother me. I was a fool to talk about it, but I was still thinking of the idea, believing it was the only key to the turbulence of life, when Jarvis got up and walked over to the door.

"Here he comes," he announced over his shoulder, and I stepped up behind him.

The funeral cortege was rolling down the street, creeping along under hot sunlight. Four motorcycle officers were escorting the hearse, and the nickeled grills and fittings of the automobiles in the slow line winked brightly. In front of me, Jarvis sniffed.

"They got a good day for it," he said, and amusement crept into his voice. "I'll bet that's the slowest the Hot Horse ever went in an automobile. They ought to let him drive. He'd scatter those cops like quail."

I didn't say anything, and the line crept along for thirty or forty minutes. Almost everybody we knew was in it, and we stood there watching until the last car had passed. Then I sat down.

"Strike Three," murmured Jarvis in a low voice, and flipped his hand out toward the empty street.

It was short, but it was his own service and I thought it better than the weeping entourage that had just gone by. While we sat there, avoiding each other's eyes, the wind picked up and rustling gusts of warm rain slapped at the walls of the office.

18

MUMFORD'S sudden departure slowed us down. For awhile, we conducted ourselves with admirable restraint and modesty. In the mornings we tried to sell Mirrolites, and in the afternoons we played golf, tennis, or swam. Jarvis put a large sign over the doorway of the office reading "Notice! There Will Be No More Whiskey Drinking Here. Signed, C. Jarvis." Fred still got drunk two or three times a week, but usually at night and away from the office. Jarvis' tongue was not as sharp as it had been, and I went to church twice with my family. It was, in truth, a renaissance, but it couldn't last. Soon we were back to normal, and the tempo of the Mirrolite proceeded.

They were fluid weeks. The time telescoped itself into periods of waking and drinking and laughing. It was a good time, spaced between aching heads, and we lost count of the days. This day would be up on the toe to smash a tennis ball and send it, hard driven and oblong from force, just over the net cord, and the next day would be golf, the slight shock of catching one on the magic spot and driving it out of sight. Not one of the lofty boomers, but the met ball that went off low from the tee and lifted. There were slices and hooks, too, but every third hole there was that good ball headed for Oklahoma or that sandy explosion that stopped pin-high. As I say, it was a good time. After our workouts, we would retreat into the grill and have a high one on the fourth hole birdie or the third consecutive ace.

Because we could do it. The whiskey was in us like a fever, but we could do it. Jarvis holed out his spoon shot on the first hole for an eagle two and it was club news. I got that clean loose lift in my shoulder and smashed a few into the backhand corner of the service court, and the crowd drifted down off the club veranda to watch me work. They were not disappointed. I spun the ball deep, followed it to the net; the return found me crouched and the half-volley bit into the base line. It was nice. Circus work, if you like, but satisfying, with the power flowing through the shoulders into every shot.

And it was definite. We weren't sure about God, but a birdie was something on a score-card, something witnessed, and a savage overhead was something to remember and grin about, just before sleep. The water was home to us. We floated in the green depths of the pool like animals grown easily into a new element. Jarvis took his two-and-a-half off the high tower like a human pinwheel, and we both floated and raced like porpoises. It would be nearly twilight, with the supper crowd gathered on the lawn, and Cavin and I would go up and amaze the common people. He would sit in a chair, on the thirty foot tower, and I would pretend I was knocking him off. Very slowly he would leave the platform, a tanned seal turning in a wicker chair, and halfway down, he would flip free and slice into the water ahead of the clumsy chair. Then would the matrons gasp and the business men smile at homegrown adventure. The warmup dances came and went and we were gripped in the somnolent passage of summer time. Five weeks went by. . . .

Perry often dropped in on us at the office, and made conversation through the sultry days. He would sit on the desk, and, swinging his booted feet, ask us innumerable questions. Nothing was alien to his search for knowledge, and he would go about for days repeating a snatch of verse. For awhile it was Cynara, and he would wander through the rooms, his light hair over his eyes, intoning softly, "I have been faithful to thee . . . in my own fashion . . . I am desolate and sick."

It wasn't true, of course, because he was not faithful to anything. On one particular afternoon, he was declaiming over Caesar's body, striding up and down before the populace, when Cavin looked up from his fingernails and shook his head sadly.

"Perry," he asked, "why don't you get a job, working?"

Perry returned from Rome. He didn't know what to say, and one hand went up to ruffle his straw-colored mop. Then he brightened visibly.

"I can't," he answered solemnly. "I got No. 5 hands, and they cramp on me." He spread the faulty hands before us apologetically, and Cavin shook his head again.

We didn't see Rick, but Garvey passed through on his way to Houston and told us his father had paid the packing company. Wilfred didn't stay long, and he didn't stay still while he was there. It was impossible for him to relax, or to carry the meaning of one sentence over to the next one. His tall, fidgety frame, his globular head with the thinning hair, and the nervous adventure in his bearing were things that set him apart.

He went on after a few days of visiting, and we didn't hear from him again, but as long as I live the memory of Wilfred Garvey will keep one corner of my heart filled with springtime. He tilted his lance at the capitalistic windmills with mad abandon, and although he was forever a loser, he never lost his zest. He was the nearest thing to a one man revolution I shall ever be privileged to witness, and down to the very last, he viewed us all with a jaundiced eye and sincerely believed that he was a business man who had been trapped by high school boys. He borrowed four dollars the day he left, and, as he reached the door, turned for a final bit of advice. He was carrying a scuffed brown bag with a rope tied around it; he wore a purple corduroy jacket, a wide black belt with silver conchas set in it, and an orange silk handkerchief was knotted at his throat. The knees of his tan whipcord pants were baggy and his boots dusty, as befits the traveller.

"Perry," he admonished, "you better sell that stuff you got. Them cattle just won't hold the money together."

He vanished, but came bursting back through the door and solemnly shook hands with all of us. He didn't look in our faces, just held out his hand and stared at the floor. When the parting amenities had been observed, he bustled back through the door and we heard his boots clicking swiftly up the drive. His last remark was in character, for the cattle he had cautioned Perry about made seven hundred dollars profit.

That afternoon, Cavin and I were playing golf when one of the bar boys caught us on the eighth green. The blackamoor came loping down the fairway with his white coat flying.

"Mr. Jimble," he called out, "they wants you on the phone up to the club." He paused for breath, his black face glistening. "It a lady, an' she say it mos' important."

Walking back to the clubhouse, I talked to the negro and wondered who could be calling. It was Lucille and she was frightened. Her voice came to me with a husky quality.

"George?" she asked. I was listening to the tightness of her tone, and she said again, "George Jimble?"

"Yes?"

"I've got to see you," she said in a breathless voice, and a hammer of doubt went swinging through my mind. Not to me, I thought; other people, but not me. This is pure slapstick, I said to myself.

"Where are you?" I asked.

"At home, but the family's gone to Dallas. Can you come right over?"

"I'll be there in five minutes," I answered, and hung up the telephone. Walking through the grill room, I told one of the waiters to tell Cavin that I had been called away. When I pushed through the door and out into the full sunshine, apprehension was an icy rash down the back of my neck. The gravel in the courtyard whispered harshly as I swung the car around and whipped between the high stone gates. Four nursemaids were chattering on the corner, their perambulators standing side by side, and a negro was walking a Great Dane down the sidewalk.

She was standing on the stairway when I opened the door and came into the quiet hall. The yellow sweater and dark skirt made her seem like a portrait of a young lady, stricken still with one hand on the stair post. Her eyes were dark in shadow, and I stood below, looking up at her. In the back of the house, a clock whispered out the hour in soft chimes, and a dog barked outside someplace. Her presence filled the hall, and, although I was too far away to smell it, the scent of her cool young body welled up in my nostrils and intermingled with the jangling discords of fear.

"I couldn't get here any sooner," I said slowly, and my voice was strange in the hall. I moved toward her, and the spikes of my golf shoes scraped on the parquet floor. She came down the stairs lightly, and I followed her into the living room. There she sank on a couch, and I lighted a cigarette and handed it to her. She took it in silence.

"Is it that solemn?" I asked, attempting a lighter tone, but it was a dismal failure for she crumpled on the chintz couch. The skirt twisted away from her slender legs almost to the hip, but there was no leap of desire in all my body.

"Yes," she said in a muffled voice, her dark hair flung across her arms, "yes, I think it's that bad."

There was a hum of voices outside on the walk, and I straightened up. The dog barked again, and after a minute the voices faded away. A mirror with red lacquered edges was hanging on the wall, and I looked into it, glanced away quickly. Just then, I didn't like the guy in it very much. The sun streamed through the partially drawn blinds, and I stood there over her.

"How long?" I asked, and she sat up. Her eyes were troubled, but she hadn't cried.

"How long?" She was vague. She didn't understand.

"How long since you knew?"

She looked straight at me and threw back her hair. "I've passed two periods," she said, and the ashes fell from my cigarette to the floor.

I blew them away. It was no great feat; I only leaned down and blew on them and they fled across the polished surface of the floor. It was as easy as that. What I had to do next was a trifle harder. As I was forming words, she spoke again.

"I'm not engaged anymore," she said. She had no makeup on, and, framed in the dark hair, her face was a seraphic oval, unlined and clear.

"Oh, yes you are," I answered. "You are engaged again. I love you."

Every word fell in the quiet room like a butcher whaling his cleaver into a side of meat. It was bald, but it was the best I could do.

"I love you," I repeated, as though I must remember that I loved her.

She lifted her bare arms and put one of them to my lips. I kissed it in the soft flesh of the elbow, and she drew one hand across my forehead. It was a cool hand; there was a light film of moisture on the palm of it, and the way she touched me was womanly. She was smiling, and the gentle part of her lips slashed at me.

"Not that way," she said quietly. "Not ever in the world like that."

She was gallantry, and I shook suddenly, wondering what I would bring per pound for catfish bait. My eyes ached with tension.

"So?" It was a foolish question, for both of us knew.

"We must do the best we can," she answered simply and got up, still smiling. "I will wait to hear from you."

That damned dog barked again outside, and I picked up my hat, turned it in my hands.

"You would have to be gone three or four days . . ."

She came up close and kissed me. I put my arms around her and we stood there locked in barricade against fear. The grace of her, the feel of her against me, and the clean fragrance of her hair came into my consciousness and became inseparable with the ugly thing that was already there.

"It doesn't matter," she said, and I could feel her lips moving against my chest. "We must do the best we can."

I kissed her on the mouth hard, not in passion but in reassurance, and then I walked out the door. I looked for that vocal dog, but he was gone and the motor of my car wouldn't turn over. As the starter ground beneath my toe, I realized that I was soaked in sweat.

19

THE office was dark when I drove up, but Fred and Cavin were sitting inside. Cavin still had on his golf clothes. They weren't doing anything, just sitting in the near darkness. A quart bottle was on the table, and I glanced around for the white blur of the no-drinking sign. It was gone. Fred was crooning that it wasn't a rare and magic perfume, that it was just love in bloom, and his sad voice sounded wonderfully contented. Since I was outnumbered, I took a drink, a long one, and it flowed warmly down my throat. For a second, nothing happened. Then it took hold and a solid heated circle flooded out from the bottom of my stomach and dissolved a part of the quivering there. The next one was even better.

"Why the twilight service?" I asked.

Jarvis was drumming an accompaniment to Fred's song, tapping his fingers on the arm of a chair. He was sitting sprawled out and I could see his smooth profile. In the dusk, he looked like a brooding prince of darkness.

"Oh, hello, Jimble," he said irritably. "It's somebody's anniversary." His voice was slurred. "And we are hoping they have the rent paid, and are frighteningly happy." He paused, and there was no sound save Fred's soft harmonizing. "How was Lucille?" asked

Cavin suddenly.

"She's been better," I answered, and poured another drink, turning something over in my mind. Jarvis swung around to look at me.

"How do you mean, she's been better?"

He was alert. The wind blew in cool, and I went over to shut the window. As I pulled on it, I spoke over my shoulder.

"She's been better," I said angrily. "Right now she's pregnant."

Jarvis made no sound behind me, and Bradley sang a few more bars, his voice finally dwindling down to stillness.

"What did you say?" he asked.

Jarvis got up from the chair. "The jam is on . . . the jam is on . . . the jam is on . . ." he chanted in a low excited voice, and came up before me. "How long?" he whispered, "how long gone?" He was still chanting. I held up two fingers and he crossed himself.

Bradley said, "This is too much," took a drink out of the bottle, and started toward the door. "I think I'll go home and get a bite to eat," he said.

Jarvis was still standing in front of me. "Stick around, Fred," he murmured. "I'm going out and knock over a bank in a little while."

Bradley stood in the doorway looking at his hands. "No," he said, "I think I'll just run on home and get a bite to eat." His tone was thoughtful. "But you can count on me . . ." His voice trailed off and he stepped out the door.

Jarvis flipped on the light, and the glare from the naked bulb lanced into my eyes. Then he pushed the bottle over toward me.

"Marriage?" he asked. I knew he was enjoying it, like he remembered the time I kicked him on the hand when he was stealing the last bottle of beer.

"No," I answered him harshly. "Not marriage. The Claw."

That moved him. I had known it would. His handsome face went sliding back into the shadows when he flinched. He bared his even teeth and licked his lips.

"Jesus," he said slowly, and then, "Holy Jumping Jesus."

I was sick and said nothing, sitting there until the nausea had worn away. My head felt light and very distant. Jarvis leaned in under the fan of yellow light, and I noticed the way his dark hair curled up in the back.

"Maybe," he said deliberately, "she's playing you for a sucker. After all, this Harold—"

When I hit him, his bent head bobbed like a float on a fishing line, and a smear of blood crawled down from the corner of his mouth. I was sitting there with bedlam loose in my head when he took out a silk handkerchief and wiped the blood away.

"Well," he said carefully, testing a tooth, "maybe not."

For awhile we sat there locked in the silence, staring at nothing and listening to the wind put weak crying tongues around the walls of the office. They were the voices of panic to me, and I took another drink, but this time the nausea didn't go away at all. When I had finished vomiting, I walked into the bathroom and washed my mouth out but my teeth still felt dirty. I cleared my throat several times and spat, realizing that Jarvis was watching me.

"Yes, you bastard," I said, "I'm caught in the switch. And I've got to have three hundred dollars."

He didn't flex a muscle. He had his chin on the back of a chair, and was regarding me thoughtfully.

"That much?" he asked.

"That much, yes."

"But I know a guy . . ."

"And I know a guy too," I broke in, "but that guy's not good enough. This one has got to be letter perfect, and I need three hundred dollars."

"Well, I hope you get it." He stood up and stretched. "But let's go over to Burton's place and sit around awhile."

Burton was his brother-in-law. I didn't want to go home because I was half drunk, so I carefully put the cork back in the bottle and we locked the office door.

Lights were blazing in the house when we arrived, and John Burton came to greet us. He was a large blond man in his middle thirties and he smelled faintly of bay rum. Annabel, his wife and Cavin's sister, was dark and intense; she cursed us lightly and shook my hand. As we stood there murmuring pleasantries, I was struck by the similarity between Cavin and the explosive little woman beside him. Except for her eyes, which were smudged by excess, they might have been twins. I was also acutely conscious of the quart bottle bulking in my pocket. Annabel looked down at it.

"How nice," she said, without smiling, and turned to her husband. "John, take the boys back and mix them a drink. In the kitchen."

Behind her, I could see people moving about in the next room. Quite a number of them, and their laughter was constrained but interesting. However we didn't go toward them; we followed the big man back through another door and into the kitchen. Annabel vanished into the more crowded room.

Burton took the cork out of our bottle and smelled it, shaking his head appreciatively. "Well boys," he asked jocularly, "how do you want your poison?" I could see that Burton was going to be too pleasant. Cavin and I said "straight" in unison, and all three of us had a good laugh.

It was a very modern kitchen, gleaming with porcelain. Dark red linoleum was on the floor, and the fittings of the sleek stove shone under the indirect lighting. Little cupboards and crannies were myriad and convenient, and the icebox was moulded into the back wall. As I fondled my drink, the box sent out a soft whirring that said it was on the job all right. The whole kitchen was spotted with electric plugs, and so filled with labor saving devices that the woman who lived in it had nothing to do but sit around and develop neuroses. It was too damned efficient, and I stared at its spotless wonder gloomily. Jarvis was perched on one side of the sink.

"How's business?" he asked John, and I groaned inwardly. As I lifted my drink, John took an explanatory stance, like a show horse, and looked very thoughtful.

"Well, Cavin," he said, "we've been pretty busy." He sipped from his glass and considered further. "Yessir," he went on conclusively, "we've been pretty busy."

I wondered what kind of business he was in, but I didn't push it. Cavin poured himself another drink, and I handed him my glass. The lights were beginning to go a little fuzzy on me. Cavin handed my refilled glass back, and asked John if he had been out to the camp lately. John, a florid man with a flushed face, considered that matter for a moment.

"No," he said, "I've just been so damned busy I haven't had time to go out. Like to, but no time. I've got that damned camp insured for twelve thousand dollars, and I haven't been out there in eight months." He paused and squinted down in his glass, as though berating himself for having such a fine camp and then never using it.

"Yes, I guess you have been pretty busy," Cavin said idly, and John laughed.

"Sure have," he intoned. "Be a saving proposition if that damned thing burned down, the way business is." He laughed again, an abdominal rumbling.

I could be just as jocular as he could, and something was stirring in the back of my mind. "Be worth a couple of thousand to you, hunh?"

"Oh, easy that, easy that . . ." He was laughing heavily and Cavin looked over at me. "You planning to burn it down?" asked John. He was genuinely and laboriously amused and my eyes narrowed.

"Two thousand dollars is in no way hay," I said, and he laughed some more. The lights were fuzzier than ever, and Jarvis came off the sink with one twist. Back of my eyes, deep in my brain, I could see Lucille standing on those stairs, poised and silent.

"I may take you up on that," I said slowly, and a look of annoyance passed over John's face, as though we had already talked too much about it. That was the point when I misjudged him.

"Well, just let me know," he answered petulantly, and started mixing himself another drink. He worked over it as hard as a man building a bridge, and he used at least seven ingredients. It seemed a complex way to transport alcohol to the stomach. Jarvis was watching me carefully.

"Now, Jimble!" he began, and was about to say something else when John turned around and asked us if we wouldn't like to go in and meet the folks. I said that we weren't dressed and he insisted, but his heart wasn't in it. Cavin picked up the bottle, and we went out the front door with the big man's strident goodbye's following us. They ceased abruptly when the door closed, and Cavin tilted his hat and looked at me. He didn't say a word for about three blocks.

"Now listen—" he began, but I cut in on him.

"Two g's," I said softly, "two whole g's."

He started to speak again, but I told him to shut up, and we pulled into a filling station. A kid in a dirty uniform came out of the door with that stock smile on his face.

"Five gallons of ethyl in a can," I told him and Jarvis quivered. The boy looked at me as if I were drunk and I looked back as if I weren't. He went away, and I handed the bottle to Jarvis. He sucked on the neck of it for quite a while.

"I don't like it," he said in a choked voice.

My head was unsteady. "I don't like it either, but what the hell?"

Jarvis looked at me for a long time. Then he took another drink and slumped down in the seat, shutting his eyes. "What the hell?" he asked aimlessly.

The boy came back and put the can in the back seat. When I was paying him, he asked me if I intended to bring the can back. I told him I was, and paid a deposit. Then we went across town and out the lake road. It was a starless night and the whole sky was overcast. Jarvis was still slumped down in the seat, and he took several more pulls at the bottle. Finally he straightened up, and a rough burr of excitement was in his voice.

"It don't make a damn," he whispered, and we went plunging down the wide road.

20

A RINGING noise tugged me out of sleep, a long persistent ringing that would not stop. Sunlight struck through the windows and gilded the room. As I shook my head and looked around, I was pleasantly surprised to see that it was my room, in my home. That same whiskey smell was heavy in my nose and my face ached. It felt like old parchment, and a crusty paste rimed my lips. Gradually I came to realize that the telephone in the hall was doing the ringing. It was not one of those things you see in a blinding flash. I just lay there with my head pounding and the telephone kept up its insistent clamor and before long I knew what was the matter.

It was Jarvis, and he had aged. "Say," he whispered thinly, "Burton's camp burned down last night."

I didn't know what course to take so I decided to stay in the middle of the road.

"What camp?" I asked him. He wasn't expecting that. "And how do I know you're not a Japanese spy? I was bowling all night long with some close friends, and I can prove every lying word of it."

Jarvis was one with the silence. "You know goddamned well what camp," he said finally.

"If you can't keep a civil tongue in your head, Cavin," I said, "I shall have to get back in bed." It was a rhyme and I repeated it several times. All the time I was searching through the pockets of my dressing gown for a cigarette, but I couldn't find one. It was a lack.

"Well, anyway," went on Jarvis, bitterly, "we burned the bastard down to the very bricks, and Burton threw a screaming running fit and called in the insurance men."

"He did what?"

"He called in the insurance men and told them all about it."

I told him to wait a minute and he asked me where I was going.

"If I can't find any arsenic," I said coldly, "I am going to get a cigarette to smoke."

I put the phone down and went back into my room. There was one left, but it was crumpled. I struck a match and lighted it, wondering whether I could make the trip back to the phone. It was tough, but I did it.

"Jarvis," I said crisply, and he grunted, "Jarvis, what is the situation?"

"It's a bitch," he answered. "You better come over here."

I told him I would, and went back to take a cold shower. Standing under the water, I thought of Lucille, the laws governing arson in the State of Texas, and how proud my family was going to be. As I dressed, I thought about murdering Pearl, the cook, and making everything come out even. I could hear her moving around down in the kitchen, but I decided against it principally because she was a big woman and I feared I couldn't kill her if I tried. She was kneading dough when I walked through the kitchen, and she lifted her broad black face.

"Doesn't you want some breakfast?"

"No, Pearl," I answered gaily, "no breakfast this morning, but isn't it a wonderful day to be glad in?"

"Sho is!" she beamed, and I went out the back door to the garage.

They were sitting in Cavin's living room when I got there. His father was slumped down in a chair and had his head well held. Burton was pacing up and down one corner of the room, and the two insurance men were sitting gingerly on the edge of the couch. A general air of solemnity prevailed, and Cavin had his back to the company. He was staring into the fireplace.

When I opened the door, he looked around at me without enthusiasm. "Mr. Briggs," he said, waving his hand airily, "and Mr. Collier."

I shook hands with Mr. Briggs and then with Mr. Collier. Mr. Collier had a vinegary looking face. I guess he was the richer of the two and worried more.

"Jimble," he said in a rasping voice, "this is a terrible thing."

"Yes, sir, it is."

Cavin's father lifted up his head. "How in the name of God could you ever do such a stupid thing?" he asked, with all the sorrow of the world in his voice. I said that I didn't know, that I guessed we had been drunk.

Burton was still pacing up and down and as near as I could figure it he had reeled off at least a mile and a half since I had come in, and never moved over twenty feet in a straight line. His eyes were bloodshot and his whole air dejected. While I was watching him, Mr. Briggs stood up and hemmed and hawed through a ten minute oration on the insurance angles of the case.

"We cannot, of course," he intoned, "accept any claim, but there is also to be considered the more serious, or criminal, aspect. . . ."

He droned on interminably and Mr. Collier sat beside him puffing on a cigar and nodding like a dyspeptic Buddha. A radio was turned to dance music, and without thinking I began to tap my feet. When I did, Mr. Briggs turned and eyed me reproachfully, so I kept still, remembering the time I had visited the State Penitentiary and hoping that if we were sent up, Jarvis would get a uniform that didn't fit. That, to him, would be more painful than the actual incarceration.

Mr. Briggs' voice wandered on sorrowfully in the stillness, and Burton turned another fast quarter back of me. Cavin looked over at me, rather morosely I must admit, and my gesture indicating stripes on a prison uniform was received by him in unblinking silence. Finally Mr. Briggs ran down, and he and Collier began to talk to Mr. Jarvis in low tones. Burton went over to join them and as he came up, Mr. Jarvis got angry.

"You can't tell me John Burton didn't instigate this thing," he shouted. "Those boys wouldn't go out and deliberately do a thing like that." He was red in the face, and he stepped back from the other men and glared at his son-in-law.

"Gentlemen, gentlemen," soothed Mr. Collier, "there is no need for any of us to lose our heads. The boys just had a little too much and did something foolish, so let's see if we can't straighten it out."

I decided that I liked Mr. Collier, but Cavin's father was shouting again.

"You're damned right they did, but he made them do it!" He pointed at Burton and his finger was trembling. When I spoke, they all wheeled around.

"If you really want to know why we did it," I said, "we did it for two thousand bucks, but Burton didn't tack our feet to the floor and funnel any whiskey in us, and he didn't know we were levelling with him about torching the joint. He had nothing to do with it." I was sore at Mr. Jarvis. "Check up, gentlemen, check up. Do you think he would have us burn the place down and then call you in as soon as he heard about it?"

This was a point they had not considered and while they were mulling it over, I told Cavin I wanted a drink of water. I wasn't lying about it; I really needed one. Mr. Jarvis had withdrawn into a moody silence, and the others were whispering. When we were in the kitchen, I drank the glass of water that Cavin handed me.

"See this?" he asked, and pointed to his face. All his eyebrows and lashes were gone, and salve was spread on his forehead.

"What happened?"

"Last night when you threw that match," he said, "a wall of fire ten feet high jumped out and got me."

He had a peeled look, and I was still laughing at his despoiled beauty when Burton came to the door and called us.

The gentlemen had decided that, with some fixing in the District Attorney's office, the thing could be hushed up. There were several worthy speeches made and I tried to look contrite but my head was paining me too badly for a genuine impression. In the speeches, they inevitably referred to the disaster as "this regrettable affair" or "this lamentable incident," and I wished they would come right out once and say "this fire" but they never did. They elaborated on the nearness of prison walls, and after we had, supposedly, shuddered at that ominous prospect, they called us both fine boys and predicted that we would go far. It was strictly copy-book and the old routine and when they were done with it, the insurance men got up and left. I walked over to Burton and said I was sorry about it. He shook hands and was polite, but he watched me with wariness, and I don't think he trusted me entirely. I could still smell the bay rum clinging to him, and as I walked out of the house I was thinking about the two thousand dollars we hadn't collected. A negro man in overalls was cutting the grass and the trees were in full foliage, so I told myself to be of good cheer, that the world was full of new life. But that thought swept Lucille back into my mind and I stepped off the porch shakily, counting on my fingers like an idiot and panic howling in my head.

21

TWO days later I got on an early train and went to San Antonio. The three hundred dollars I had borrowed from my uncle was snug on my hip, and when I had checked in at a hotel, I consulted the slip of paper in my pocket. A name and building number were written on it, and I memorized them and burned the paper. Then I took a shower, and, after dressing in a light suit, went down the quiet hall. The elevator boy was Mexican; he spoke with a liquid accent, and when I asked him where the Spartan Building was, he broke into a torrent of explanation. I slowed him down some.

"Three blocks south and one block east. That it?"

His teeth were startling white. "Si, si," he smiled, and when we got downstairs I bought cigarettes and walked down the street according to his directions. The building was a big one, set in the very heart of the city. In its lobby, I studied the directory board until I came to the name I wanted. It was on the seventeenth floor.

An old woman was typing in the outer office. She had false teeth, and when she looked up I could see part of the bright gums nestling behind her drawn mouth.

"I'd like to see the doctor," I said.

She was wary; her eyes roamed over me. "For what purpose?"

she asked. She whistled a little bit when she talked.

"I'd like to see the doctor himself," I said, trying not to get angry. "Dr. Harcort sent me."

She got up and bustled into the other room. I could hear her murmuring inside, and then she came back out and stood by the door, motioning for me to go in. I had the irrational thought that she was far too old to be a receptionist, but I walked past her and shut the door back of me.

"Dr. Rucker?" I asked.

There was a gnome behind the desk, a gnome with thick glasses over its eyes, and the eyes were observing me carefully.

"I am Dr. Rucker," said the figure, and then the nutcracker chin and sharp nose went down as he waved at a chair.

"I was sent by Dr. Harcort," I said slowly.

"Yes?" His voice was low and noncommital.

"I'm in some trouble, Doctor. I thought perhaps you could help me. Here is a letter I have for you."

I took the envelope out of my breast pocket and put it on the desk. When his hands came up over the shining surface, I started involuntarily, for they were tremendously large and the fingers were thick and spatulate. Veins lined them darkly, and muscle layers ridged up between the fingers. When he had finished reading the letter, he looked up.

"Your wife?"

I was well rehearsed. "Yes, sir," I said, "we've been married for a little over a year."

"Is she here?" He was leaning forward, as though he might spring on me without warning if he found a flaw in my story.

"No, sir," I said, "I came down first to make the arrangements."

He didn't say anything for a long time, just looked at me.

"It might be dangerous," he piped out suddenly. "I'll have to examine her, or have a nurse do it. If she's healthy, I'll take her, but you must sign a release . . ." He drummed on the desk. "Is she big?"

"No, sir, not very."

I lighted a cigarette and he ducked and started burrowing in the desk drawers, coming up with an ebony ash tray that he pushed across to me. Again I noticed his absurdly big hands.

"How far is she gone?"

"Nearly three periods," I told him, and he kept up that soft drumming on the desk.

"Late. You came late," he muttered, "but we'll try the other first."

I didn't know what the other was, but I figured I'd find out. He looked up and blinked behind the thick lenses.

"You know my fee? You are prepared to pay a nurse?"

I told him I was, and he wrote something on a slip of paper. The fountain pen looked fragile twitching in his hand, and once he looked up and asked me where I was staying. He asked me when she would be in town, and I told him that too.

"Get her here and put her to bed. Have this filled, and I'll send the nurse over early tomorrow. We'll wait long enough to see if this works, and if it doesn't, bring her here to me. The nurse will tell you. That's all."

He finished as abruptly as he had begun and sat there waiting for me to go. The light made silver ovals of his eyes, and the big hands bulged on the desk as I put the piece of paper in my pocket and turned away. He was a shrunken little man, and you could feel the tension in him. The old woman glanced up shortly as I passed through, and then went back to her filing cabinet. As I put my hat on, I wondered how many women had passed through that door, how many he had put those huge hands on. The thought was heavy and unsettling in my mind as I stepped out of the elevator to the sunny street and sucked in a deep breath of fresh air.

Lucille came down the next day. She had told her family that she was visiting friends over the week-end, and there was one agonizing stretch between telephone calls when it looked as if she couldn't come at all. During that interim, I paced the hotel room and smoked several thousand cigarettes, but the difficulty was arranged and she came in on the morning train. The hotel desk had been late in waking me, and she was standing in the great concourse of the station when I got there, standing with her luggage piled around her feet and a ridiculously long feather slanting out of her hat. She was watching the crowd, the bright feather turning as she moved, and I saw her as soon as I burst through the station doors. When I came in, she walked over to meet me with a swinging stride, her body trim in a tailored suit. I caught her by the elbows and kissed her bright mouth.

"I thought you had gone to China," she said, and I grinned down at her.

When I had arranged for the luggage, we walked outside and got a cab. I told her what the plans were, and she put her hands in mine. For the rest of the way we were silent.

At the hotel, we went up to the room I had engaged for her. It was next to mine, and, while she bathed, I called Dr. Rucker. When the connection had been made, I told him we were ready for the nurse.

"Has she been sick at the stomach?" he grated. I told him to wait, and crossed over to the bathroom door.

"You been sick at the stomach?" I asked, and when she answered no I retraced my steps. She was splashing in the tub.

"No sickness," I reported, and the doctor grunted.

"All right," he said. "The nurse will be there before noon. Did you get the material?"

"Yes."

"Good. Have the nurse call me tomorrow." And he hung up abruptly.

I was reading the morning paper when she came out of the bathroom and began to comb her wet hair. She wore a blue negligee and blue mules. Standing like that before the mirror, with her head thrown back, she seemed amazingly smaller. When the comb caught in a snarl of the dark hair, she said "damnation!" in a low voice.

"Tsk . . . tsk," I murmured from my chair, and she looked around and smiled. Framed in the cascading wings of hair, her face was tranquil, and when she sat down at the little dressing table, the negligee slid away from her tanned legs. I dived back into the paper, but the neat black legend on the pages wouldn't make sense. I affected a matter-of-fact tone.

"Nurse won't be here until noon," I said gruffly, and heaved up from my chair. "Think I'll go down and get a shave." I looked across at her and fingered my chin. I didn't need a shave very much.

She was watching me in the round mirror, smiling at me as though I were a child. The negligee whispered as she crossed and stood beneath my shoulder, and I was conscious again of how small she was without high heels. Her hair was still damp, and the clean woman smell was on her. As I looked down, she tapped me lightly on the shoulder.

"You don't have to run away," she said. "The horse is gone."

Traffic passed on the street below, and a telephone jangled in a room down the hall. It rang for several minutes, a loud imperative summons, and then died out. Her waist was slender; I could put my hands almost around it, and I was keenly aware of her litheness under the gown. Her kiss was soft and searching, an insinuating pleasure that moved warmth over my mouth and shook me. The touch of her naked body shocked my hands and shook a fever into my head. Desire stiffened in me like wonder, and I put her down on the bed, looked at her rounded loveliness. All of a sudden, something was in my throat, strangling me.

"This is it," I said huskily, drinking in the sight of her for remembrance against the time when I should grow old and die. "This is all we've got. . . ."

And then I took off my readymade suit and my sanforized shirt and my wrinkleproof tie and lay down beside her. For a little while, there on the bed, we forgot fear and everything else. For a little while, the two of us were locked in one strong current.

Later, when we were smoking, I tangled my hand in her hair and pulled her head over on my shoulder, so that I could see the line of her face, quiet in repose, just below my chin.

"Nobody ever told me," I said, "that it could be this good."

Her eyelashes flickered upward swiftly and her pale mouth twisted.

"Is it the best way?" she asked me suddenly.

"No," I said, "it's not the best way, but it's the only way we've got. We've got to piece it all together like a broken pattern, out of dirty snickers and whispered jokes. It's the best damned thing we've got, and yet we've got to handle it and juggle it and abuse it and stumble along blindly until we begin to get an idea what it's all about."

She twisted again and sighed. My hand was lying along her throat and I could feel a faint pulsing there.

"I can remember," she said shyly, "some books one of the girls at school had. Terrible books. You know the kind I mean?"

"Yes," I said. "I know."

"And they were all so . . ." She spread her slender hands and gestured helplessly. "So . . . spoiled by clothes and smiles." She looked up at me again. "And that's not right, is it?" She put a cool palm against my mouth. "Because it can be . . . so sweet."

"Yes," I said, kissing the hand, "it can be sweet."

Her hand was still at my mouth when a knock came on the door. Her head was still pillowed in my arms and her eyes were clear. They moved me, seemed to know something that I didn't know, and I leaned over and kissed her again, from the heels.

"Thanks," I said, and began to dress. Her eyes followed me steadily, and I realized with a start that, for the first time, I had not wanted to leave her.

The nurse was at the door, and she was growing impatient when I finally opened it. She was a middleaged woman in a shapeless hat, and she wore a brown dress with a simple lace collar. When I gave her the bottles and remedies I had bought, she went into the bathroom with them, like a plodding alchemist about to work miracles. Lucille beckoned to me from the bed, and I walked over. Her white arms snaked up and she kissed me very hard.

"I'll be downstairs," I said. "Good luck."

"I'll do my damndest," she answered, and made a mock heroic face. "Come back soon."

"All right." I turned and walked out the door, her enchantment still bemusing me. The lobby was almost deserted, but I bought a paper and sat down to read it. It took me several minutes to realize that it was the same paper I had been reading upstairs, and beyond the potted palms at the far end of the lobby, I could see stairs going down and a small neon sign that said "Bar." I sat there looking at the sign, not moving, thinking about Lucille and tightening up. I sat there, but I wanted more than anything in the world to go moving toward that sign, the one that said "Bar." Finally I heaved up, went outside, and walked into a movie. It was a very bad show, and I sat through most of it with my eyes shut and my hands pressed to my temples.

Lucille was quiet in the big double bed when I went back up, and the nurse had removed that battered felt hat. She was rocking by the bed, and her face was a stolid mask. I walked over and took one of Lucille's hands, lifted it with spread fingers. Framed in the pillow, her face was dusky warmth, the core and heart of the room.

"What was it you gave her?" I asked the nurse. She kept on rocking. Words were hard for her to find.

"A strong . . . purgative . . . laxative," she grumbled. "Some other things you wouldn't . . . know the names of . . ." She paused and sighed heavily. "Sometimes it makes them . . . miscarry. Not . . . all the time."

I bent down and put my head against the curve of Lucille's throat, the hollow that was flushed with warmth. Her heart pulsed faintly next to my cheek, and she brought her free arm over and put it back of my head. The nurse rocked on and afternoon whistles shrieked outside. I was bent so when the nurse spoke again.

"You had best . . . not excite her."

"All right." I straightened up from the bed, and stroked her hair in leaving. Her mouth was working slightly, and a light mist clouded her eyelids. "How long before we can tell about this?" I asked the nurse.

"Tomorrow morning."

"This Rucker," I went on, impatience edging up in me. "He's all right, isn't he?"

She smoothed the folds of her dress. "He's done a whole lot of them . . . he should know . . . how," she said, and I walked over to sit on the lounge, thinking what a fool I was to have asked the question in front of Lucille.

It was darkening outside, and the lowering light melted softly around the white battlements and narrow streets of San Antonio. Across the serrated ranks of the buildings, I saw the deep masses of greenery that marked a park, and I knew the Alamo would be just beyond. I thought of shadowy heroes footing across its dusty floors, puking up their guts and sweating in that tiny corner of Texas, firing their long rifles vengefully and effectually against the onrushing wave of Santa Anna's army. But it was only an old story and a cheap thrill, thinking of such unbelievable heroics against death, and my eye wavered to the street below, to the vivid splashes of color that sprang up as signs were lighted, gaily caparisoned symbols of whiskey and cereal and bread that made the roof of the town a highflung commercial fairyland. Behind me, in the darkening room, Lucille got out of bed and whispered something to the nurse, and I heard a rustling as they both went into the bathroom. Newsboys piped out Hitler's name on the street below, and their thin shoutings dwindled up and down the town. Soon Lucille came back and got in bed again. I turned around, a cigarette glowing dully at my fingertips.

"I want one," whispered Lucille faintly, and I came off the couch, not comprehending. I stood there, poised.

"She wants . . . a cigarette," said the nurse harshly, and I crossed and put the one I had between her lips. She was just a shape, but when the tip of the cigarette flared, I could see her face and it was waxen and tired.

"Can she eat?"

"No!" The nurse was low and emphatic.

"What about you?"

The woman heaved in her chair. "I brought something," she said shortly, and lapsed into silence. I remember thinking that she was the most unfriendly woman I had ever seen, and I wondered where she had concealed her luncheon. It had grown almost completely dark, and I went to the bathroom and switched the overhead light on. Then I opened the door so that a sliver of brilliance fell into the other room.

"I'll be back in a minute," I said, but Lucille was breathing quietly and the nurse rocked on without turning. It occurred to me that I might just be in the way, and I went down the hall on my toes. I couldn't shake the thought that I was in a hospital.

Down in the coffee shop, I ordered a sandwich and some milk, not particularly wanting them but trying to wear away time, trying to combat the silence that had time suspended in the room upstairs. The waitress was Mexican and she had liquid eyes, but the first flush was gone. Loveliness was not on her, and a wisdom of gringo ways was written into the way she acted. When I had ordered, she reached over for the menu and her breasts brushed my shoulder. For an instant they were soft there, an undeniable pressure, and then she turned away. Her shoes were scuffed and one of her stockings was crooked along the calf. I noticed these things and sat there sipping my water, wondering at the endless esoteric play that humanity indulges in. It was something that people went through with their hands and eyes and thought, as well as their bodies.

While I was thinking about it, a face pressed out of the darkness and peered through the front window of the coffee shop, the grotesquely drawn face of a man either very drunk or very hungry. It was pasted there on the broad window for a moment, like the substance of a disappointed ghoul, shadowed and angry, and then it melted back into the darkness. I wondered if I was seeing things, and the girl put the sandwich down in front of me. She spilled a very little bit of the milk, and began a soft bickering of apology.

"No matter," I said, and motioned her away. It didn't take but a minute to eat the sandwich, and I left a tip and got up. As I paused at the cashier's desk, I could see the waitress standing in the back of the room, her dark eyes on me, but I pushed out through the swinging doors to the elevator. The red bar sign burned steadily to my right, but I pressed the button and went upstairs.

I sat on the couch all night, smoking and waiting. Lucille called me once and I went over to stand by the bed and hold her hand, thankful that I had been there when she called. Her voice, in the stillness, was that of a little girl.

"It's pretty rough," she whispered, and I stroked her hair and stood there until her hand slipped out of mine. Then I went back to the couch. Four or five times, she got out of bed and went into the bathroom, the nurse padding behind her. Every time it happened, I sat there feeling my uselessness, because I had nothing to do, nothing to fight.

Shortly after three o'clock, the nurse took some sandwiches from her pocketbook and began to munch on them. Her chewing sounded steadily in the quiet room, and she must have chewed each bite fifty times. I started counting the soft snaps of her jaws but inevitably lost count. Once I went downstairs to get another package of cigarettes, but hurried back for fear Lucille might call out for me and find herself alone with that hesitant ogre of a nurse. The lobby was deserted save for the night clerk and three sleepy bellboys, and the early morning breeze was cool flowing off the street. While I was down there, a sweeper chugged down the street putting out fans of water and whirling its great brushes. I watched it pass, and went back upstairs. The bar was closed.

At five, the darkness began to pale, and in half an hour, the first cold spears of morning came into the room. My feet ached, and I was wondering whether or not to take a shower when Lucille got out of bed and went into the bathroom again. This time the nurse came out first and stood before me, arms akimbo on her hips. When she spoke, her voice was angry and pointed at me.

"She'll never do it."

I stood up and swung my shoulders.

"Why not?"

"Because she just won't. Some will and some won't . . ." She trailed off. "You oughtta thought of this."

I was too tired to argue with her. "Madame," I said curtly, "believe me, I did not plan it this way."

She turned around, muttering something about "that sweet child," and stalked back into the bathroom. I was staring out the windows, wondering at her sudden temper. Before, the sky had been grey and cold; now the sun began to flex out its bright petals, and warm light flooded into the room.

We waited until ten-thirty in the morning, but nothing happened. Then, without warning, the nurse got up and put on her battered hat.

"No good," she said, and walked across the room and out the door. Lucille was awake and smiling faintly, but her face was waxen and shadowed, especially under the eyes.

"Bad luck, Mr. Jimble," she whispered, and I walked to the telephone. Dr. Rucker answered, and I wondered where the old woman was. Fancy said she might have died in the night, or strangled on those false teeth.

"Yes?" the doctor asked.

"We had no luck at all," I answered. I heard him clucking softly.

"Bring her over," he said, and the phone clicked.

I turned around. Fear was swelling in me like a fungus, and it shunted me about like a boxcar. Her eyes were on me; she was sitting up in the bed, fluffing out her dark hair.

"It's time to go," I said, and she didn't move for a minute. Her hands paused. They were lost in the mass of hair.

"All right." She threw back the covers and swung her feet out of bed. When she had gathered up her clothes, she stepped into the bathroom, and I wondered how many times she had gone through that door.

"I'm not going to take any stockings," she called out. "I won't need them, will I?"

I raised my voice. "No, I don't think you will."

The town was busy; sounds of its bustling floated up through the windows as I waited. When she came back through the doorway, she was tugging at one hip.

"What's the girdle for?" I asked abruptly. Her eyes were wide, and I saw red streaks in them.

"I don't know. The nurse said to wear it."

She turned, and standing before the mirror, arranged the blue felt hat with the long feather in it. Her mouth was freshly painted, and she seemed to be preparing for a promenade in the park or luncheon with some of her friends. She turned around.

"Ready?" she asked brightly, and we went out of the room with our arms linked. I was conscious of my rumpled clothes and unshaven chin, but that was all. They didn't bother me greatly. We stood out in the sunshine a moment, and then I handed her into a cab. While we were gliding away, I said the other thing I had to say.

"It's not too late. If you want to stop . . . go back . . . ," but she put the palm of her hand over my mouth, and in another minute we were in front of the Spartan Building.

The quiet in the outer office was heightened by the drone of the elevators around the corner. The old woman was thumbing through some papers, and her glance wavered straight to the fifteen cent wedding ring I had handed to Lucille in the hall. She smiled slightly at us, said "good morning" so that it sounded indecent, and scuttled into the inner office. Then she came back and said the doctor was ready.

After Lucille had gone in, I sat down and tried to read a magazine. The memory of her passage through that inner door, with that jaunty feather tilted to one side, lived in my mind so vividly that the print on the page would not make sense. The cigarettes I lighted burned low and put blisters between my fingers, and once I cursed aloud. When I did, the old woman looked up from her desk with rheumy eyes and stared at me. Feet pattered and shuffled down the hall outside, and once a Mexican boy came in and dropped a folded newspaper on the desk.

Halfway through the second hour, I went down the hall and got a drink of water, wondering whether or not to go in after her, wondering if she was having a hard time. I remembered, too, the doctor's eyes, opaque and unreadable behind glasses silvered by the light, as he said, "It might be dangerous," and I saw again the huge hands bulging on the desk. I was clammy with sweat and the nerve in my cheek started jumping wildly. Let her come out, I breathed to myself, Great God Almighty, let her come out . . . I could see down the hall from where I was sitting, and a woman passed by, a young woman. Mechanically I swung around to stare at her hips and legs.

Shortly before the second hour was up, Lucille came back through the doorway, her face strained and set. She looked so much older that, at first, I did not even rise from my chair until she made a queer gesture of appeal, an aimless fluttering of her hands. She was carrying the hat, and as I came over to her, she put it on, but very carefully. We left the office. The old woman did not look up from her papers, and the hall outside was crowded with people coming back from lunch. I led her through them to the elevators, in a fury to get away from the people and back to the friendly quiet of the hotel room. She stopped suddenly and stood still, with the throng streaming around her.

"Don't go fast," she said. The paint was gone from her lips and they were sallow. "Go slow."

They were the first words she had spoken, and when we were downstairs, at the entrance to the building, she stopped again. She smiled at me, but it was an effort.

"I'm all right," she said. "You go into the drugstore and call a cab. And get me some paregoric. I'll wait right here." She was standing with her legs very close together, and she saw my anxiety. "Go ahead," she repeated. "I'm all right."

When I had called the cab and bought the paregoric, I went back to her and we waited while the crowd eddied around us. She was standing very straight, and when the cab came I hurried her in and directed the driver. As we rolled along, she grabbed my hands and began to cry softly.

"Tell him to hurry," she said between drawn lips, "tell him to hurry, I'm bleeding . . ."

The driver looked around when I rapped on the glass. "Faster!" I shouted, and the cab jumped as he gunned it sharply. At the hotel, we got out and were lucky enough to find an elevator waiting. The room was a dusky haven, and Lucille went directly into the bathroom. Like a homing pigeon, I thought wryly. While I was standing there, the phone rang and a voice asked if I wanted the hotel desk to pay the taxi driver. I told them to pay it and put it on the bill, and I was hanging up the phone when Lucille came back into the room.

"I'm all right now," she said, not smiling. "I'm sorry I got scared."

I shifted from one foot to the other. "Was it bad?"

She nodded gravely. "Yes, it was pretty bad. I wouldn't do it again."

"You won't have to," I answered, and threw back the covers on her bed.

She was standing back of me, watching, and her stance was still strangely erect. It wasn't the way she was used to standing, and it looked awkward. I picked her up carefully and lowered her onto the bed. She sat there like a little girl, looking down at her hands, and when I started to undress her, she looked up quickly.

"No," I said. "Don't. It's all I can do. I wish there were more."

She put her hands down and I took her clothes off. She stood up while I slipped the gown over her head, and then I combed her hair and washed her face with a damp towel. When I was through, she snuggled down in the bed, and some of the tension seemed to have drained out of her face. She smiled up at me wanly, and said "thanks" in a small voice.

"It was really nothing," I answered. "We'll go home in the morning."

She looked up at me without blinking, and reached for one of my hands. The places where she kissed it were soft, but the rest of me felt seven thousand years old.

"All right," she said sleepily, "we'll go home whenever you say." Sighing, she dozed off and didn't awaken until the stars had been out a long time.

"Are you still there?" she whispered drowsily.

"Yes," I answered, "I'm still here."

I wanted a drink so badly my hands started shaking in my lap, but finally the desire passed and a cold wind blew up outside the windows. It held rain that put a thousand liquid jewels on the window panes, and the sound of its falling came into the room with a gentle hiss.

22

WHEN I got back to town, I didn't go anyplace or see anybody for a week. Then, one afternoon, I went by the Mirrolite office. Cavin and Fred were cleaning out the desk drawers and stacking the blank panels. About thirty-four were left, and a little man in a brown suit was counting them as I came in. Fred was dismantling the spray gun and boxing his drawing instruments while Jarvis enlarged on the potential wonder of the Mirrolite Company, dwelling on the exclusive residences that now boasted the product, and the many more that could be shown the light. As I came in, he turned around.

"Mr. Buchard, Mr. Jimble," he said, and eyed me closely. "Mr. Buchard is buying out the company."

The gentleman put a soft hand in mine and murmured a greeting. Fred looked up from his desk.

"How was the trip?" he asked, and Jarvis stopped talking again. Mr. Buchard went on counting the equipment.

"It was all right," I said, and sat down, rubbing my eyes. Cavin resumed his detailed story of Mirrolite possibilities. I could see Fred's face, and every time Cavin mentioned the good will we had built up, he flinched, but the brisk little man couldn't see him. I knew Fred was thinking about all the signs we had made him steal back.

"Here," said Jarvis, "is our prospect list, and this page contains the names of our customers. It might be of some help." He sniffed thoughtfully. "It's a damned shame, fellows, that we didn't have time to develop this thing."

It was magnificent. He really was sorry, and I murmured that it was certainly a shame. The little man coughed and handed Cavin a check. Then we gathered up all the stuff and took it out to his car, where he thanked us and shook hands all around before driving away.

"How much?" I asked Cavin, as the tangible assets of the Mirrolite vanished down the street.

"Strictly sacrifice," he said. "Only two hundred dollars." He pronounced it dolers, and I started laughing. We went back inside the office.

The place looked bare without the rows of blank number panels, and Bradley started cleaning out the front closet. There were, in all, thirty-seven bottles excluding beer, of which there was a case and a half. We stood there watching as Fred piled them on the floor, and both of us were smiling faintly. Bradley lifted out his sun helmet and the boy scout shorts, two thermos jugs, and a soiled scrap of feminine lingerie.

"This one," he said, holding out the dirty silk garment, "escapes me. What night was this?"

Jarvis opened the window and started throwing the bottles out. An unseen chicken squawked resentfully.

"Belonged to somebody's mother, I guess," he said, and I was laughing until the import of it came to me.

"Unfunny, Jarvis. Remarkably unfunny," I told him, and he turned to stare at me, harshness twisting his handsome face. He needed a shave, and the wind fingered through his black hair.

"Don't get upset. I'm going to the coast next week," he announced abruptly, as though that might soothe me. Fred had been talking over the telephone, leaving an order for it to be disconnected.

"Yes," he said, hanging up the receiver, "our King Cavin is going to be a great actor, going to study in a swank dramatic school."

I looked at Cavin. "So?" I said.

"So," he answered, and we were standing there when Perry came in and stared around at the stripped office.

"Bankrupt." It wasn't a question; it was a statement, and we didn't bother to straighten him out. "Where's the whiskey?" he asked, as though that was the only question of any real importance.

"Where's your wife, you nickle and dime loafer?" asked Jarvis. "Where's she?"

Perry clacked his bootheels on the floor. "Nancy, you mean?"

"What are the names of your other wives?" I asked, and he grinned.

"Oh, hell," he said, "she's got a job in the perfume department, down to the Fair Store."

Cavin was regarding him closely, and Fred turned around for a brief glimpse. Perry was unperturbed, and he cut another little fandango.

"Well, Von," I said pleasantly, "I hope you got her a good job."

"Not very." He stopped dancing and snorted. "Fourteen bucks a week . . ." He stood there stroking the back of his neck, lost in sad contemplation of the fact that his wife was forced to work for such ridiculous wages. Finally, he brightened. "Where's the cards? Let's play a little pitch."

Jarvis got the cards out of the desk, and we played a few games of pitch. After Perry had lost three games for a dollar each, I demanded an accounting, and when he produced no money, I took his watch. He was voluble in protest, and not disposed to release it, but I convinced him it would be best. When we quit playing, he owed us thirteen dollars against it. We were leaning back and stretching when I told them that I was going to Chicago. Fred moaned dismally.

"It's the end of the Mirrolite. Jarvis goin' to the coast, Rick gone, Mumford cold, and Jimble going to Chicago. What will you ever do up there?"

"Got an uncle there. Runs an advertising agency," I explained, "and he offered me a job. Don't know what I'll do, exactly."

Perry was playing solitaire, his round face absorbed. "Seems as if," he began, "we ought to pitch a minor bitch . . ."

"All right with me," I said, "just as long as I'm not the bitch pitched."

We held a rather hurried caucus on it, and Bradley ordered a quart of whiskey from Ballinger Street. When the boy came with it, we split the cost three ways, figuring four and deducting Perry's share from the watch.

Not until the first drink pooled its warmth inside me did I realize how long it had been between drinks, and when the bottle was half gone I got up and took a bath, lounging in the icy water and massaging my scalp gently. I was thrashing like a porpoise when Jarvis came to stand in the doorway. His shadow darkened the small room, and I looked up.

"How did she make it?" he asked slowly. Gravity was on his face, and concern. It was something new. I sat there looking at him with water running down me in cold lanes.

"Fine," I said. "She did all right."

He was motionless.

"That's good." He watched me for a moment and went back out. I resumed my ablutions, and when they were done, the problem of a towel became vital, but I compromised by removing most of the moisture with my shorts. Perry was telling a joke absolutely devoid of humor but sufficiently dirty, and Jarvis and Bradley rewarded him with halfhearted guffaws. Perry was aggrieved.

"That's why I miss the Hot Horse so much," he said resentfully. "The Hot Horse was a sonsabitch that would laugh at anything."

It was true. As I pulled my clothes on, I was smiling. Mumford would laugh at anything. The bath had put a glow on my body and whiskey had warmed the interior. When I had walked back into the other room, I filled a glass and tilted it. The drink sluiced down swiftly and exploded. The world was a good world, and I was glad to be alive in it. I poured another.

"My friends," I said, and bowed to them, "my charming and worthless cohorts, I give you the whiskey, that hot hard sun of hope, that beaming sun which lights the eyes of those of us who keep an overwhelming wakefulness. Gentlemen, and members of the Louse Brigade, I give you the utterly sad dissolution of the Mirrolite Company."

Shaggy-haired Fred filled his glass and held it up. Perry was mumbling something to himself, and Jarvis arose with a slight smile. Standing there in the dirty little office, we grinned at each other and had a big one on the demise of Mirrolite. We were all a trifle self conscious as we sat back down, but it was real Empire stuff for a minute. We chatted on for awhile, made plans to meet at the drug store later, and Perry and Bradley got up and left. Jarvis reminded me of the club dance that night, and I picked up the telephone and called Lucille. Luckily, she answered the phone.

"How does it go?" I asked.

Her voice was low and troubled. "All right." She paused. "George?"

"Yes?" It was growing darker, and Cavin sat back of me, a listening shape.

"I'm going to be married next week."

Behind me, Cavin lighted a cigarette, and his match scraped across the desk. My mouth felt dry.

"Good," I said. "I congratulate him."

Her voice rose again, with panic in it, as though she feared I might hang up. "But I'll be at the dance tonight. . . ."

"Good," I said. "Fine," and then I did hang up.

Jarvis reached around me and got the bottle. He didn't say anything, just took a drink and waited. The sun's last fine blood stained the far edge of the valley, but it was a fading brilliance and I knew it would be gone in a minute. The thought of its impermanence entered me and angered me. I stood up and the chair overturned.

"Why is it, Jarvis," I asked bitterly, "that I always wind up sitting in the darkness with you, and both of us boozing and moping like a pair of disgruntled ghouls?"

He laughed, a hard barking laugh. "What's the matter?" he asked.

"No matter. Only she's going to marry that pink-cheeked moronic bastard of a Harold."

"Oh," he answered softly, "oh, that's too bad. Did you want to marry her?"

"No," I said, "I suppose not."

He didn't say anything else, and when I looked out over the valley again, the sunlight was all gone, as I had known it would be. I poured a drink, and was about to take it when I turned suddenly and threw it in Jarvis' beautiful, inscrutable face. Then I poured another and drank it. Jarvis didn't move, but he smiled a little bit, and the whiskey drained down his face and put its strong reek into the air.

23

WE MET that night at the drug store, and pulled into our usual places. Altogether, there were the Perrys, Von and Nancy, Bradley and a slender girl named Ann Alice Wiggins, Jarvis and myself. While we were mixing our first drinks, a car with the back shades drawn pulled up by us. A negro was driving, and he stopped the car and sat there. He didn't sound the horn for service or get out of the car, and I was turned around watching him when one of the back shades flew up and Rick Walton put his bristling thatch out.

"Pssst! . . ." he called, with a conspiratorial air, and we all shouted with laughter. Perry shouted, "Why Rick Walton, when did you get back in town?" and Rick shuddered and withdrew into the shadowed back seat of the long car. I walked over, got in beside him, and we shook hands.

"How does it go?" I asked, and he lighted a cigarette.

"All right," he said. "How's the situation here?"

I told him all I knew, that Barney had quieted down, that Dorothy was on a South American cruise, and that he'd better have a drink.

"You look dejected," I said, and he really did, but he refused the drink.

"No more of that hard stuff," he stated flatly. "I'm through with that, and I'm leaving for school tonight. The old man wired that he figured it would be all right to go back now."

When I pressed him to come out to the dance with us, he was horrified and reproached me for suggesting it. We shook hands again, and I got out. Rick twisted to the front seat beside the driver and sat there looking at me, smiling faintly.

"If we do not meet again," I said, "why then our parting was well made. Or something tangible, something Shakespearean and doleful. Goodbye, Rick."

He spoke to the driver, who slammed the back door, and then drove away. I watched the tail light out of sight, and as I walked back toward the others it occurred to me that I had not told him I was going to Chicago. Cavin was standing outside the car when I walked up; he was pouring a drink.

"Ricky seemed a trifle agitated," he remarked.

He was pleasantly tight, and had an air of great good humor.

"Yes," I said, "he was on the lookout for Barney."

Jarvis was deprecatory. "Oh hell," he said, "that's all washed up. I'd rather not hear anything more about it."

I promised not to bother him with it any more. Bradley's date, Miss Wiggins, was doing a good deal of excited squealing inside the car, and I wondered exactly what was going on. Von Perry, who could not sing, was singing loudly, and we had still another one and went out to the dance.

The same people were there and they were doing the same things. This one wasn't formal, but we all contrived to look as formal as possible in linens and flannels and light frocks. The same drunks were barging around the floor, and the same expressions were on their faces. Some were garmouthed in lax appreciation of the music, some were grimly intent on being gay, and some were crafty and knowing, tipsily elegant. They came to the sight like a moving string of masks passing under subdued lights. As of yore, the white shoulders dipped gracefully, and the gentlemen hounded their especial favorites to the far corners. Music pulsed around them and impelled their sliding feet, and everyone was, very obviously, very happy.

While I was standing there, thrusting my chin forward and lifting my shoulders in those peculiar motions so necessary to all who stand in a stag line with any distinction, Perry appeared at one of the porch doors and beckoned to me. I walked over and found him reeling against the wall. He was overcome with laughter.

"You remember Al Barnes, that big manly bastard from Culver?" he gasped.

I nodded my head. Barnes was a muscle merchant who had been to school at Culver and in the East. I understand that, as a child, he had been very lonely and had been forced to play with himself. At any rate, he had a very patronizing way, as though he inhabited our sphere under extreme duress, having known greater joys.

Perry was killing himself. "Well," he choked out, "Barnes was up here dancing, got right pert drunk, and decided to go swimming during this last intermission. Sort of an added thrill for the ladies, you understand. . . ." That uncontrollable mirth shook him again, and he bent over and howled.

"Well?"

"Well, he went downstairs and got in his trunks. Then the bastard came rushing out of the clubhouse, tore across the grass, and went into a high arching swan dive."

"So what?" I didn't think it was that funny.

"So. . . ." Here Perry broke down again. ". . . so there wasn't any water in the pool."

I stood there, shocked at first, and then amused. "Didn't it kill him?" I asked. Perry was scornful.

"Why hell no," he said, some of his mirth subsiding. "Just dazed him. Hit the bottom and there was a couple inches of water in it. Skidded along on his nose for about ten feet, then got up and climbed out of the pool shaking his head." He savored the memory. "Didn't have much nose on him though."

Back of us, the music started again, and I watched Perry laugh but refused his proffer of a drink. He was carrying a pint bottle in his coat pocket. I asked him if he hadn't heard about repeal, and stressed the fact that it was now legal to have a bottle, but he only took a quick snort and grimaced. He may not have heard, and when he had capped the bottle, he left me to tell somebody else about Barnes' mishap. I turned around, and soon Nancy Perry came by, slender in white and with her blonde hair braided. She looked like an especially elegant Dutch Doll, and since I am partial to the low countries, I cut in on her.

We were going along nicely when I saw Lucille come in and begin to dance with Harold. She was wearing a crinoline dress of graduated blue that darkened toward the bottom and swirled around her feet. She saw me too, and smiled uncertainly before she vanished into the pack.

It took me twenty minutes to find her when I had finished dancing with Nancy Perry. She was in one of the deep recesses of the hall, and that stock look of incredible delight was on her face as she turned to me.

"Easy," I said, "you're among friends," and she smiled again, this time a softer, different way, but she didn't say anything.

People bumped us and we bumped people until the music died, and then I started across the floor. When I was at the door, she hesitated for a second; her fingertips tightened shortly in mine, but I tugged at them and she came out.

We took refuge in a corner of the dark veranda. To the east, the jagged outline of the business section sent up its sharp profile and hung its colored messages against the night sky. The golf course spread out around us, and friendly orange blurs filled the windows of the houses at its edge. The water hole was like a black mirror to our left, and as we watched, a striking fish broke its purity and jarred out silver ripples.

"I hear you are going to Chicago," she said at my elbow. I was still holding her hand.

"Yes," I answered. "And I hear you are going farther than that."

She didn't say anything then, and the wind came in and caught us in the dark corner. I kissed her on top of the head and narrowed my eyes against the wind.

"The whiskey's in me," I said slowly, "and I could promise you that I would get the stars, climb to them and tear them from their sockets. . . . But when the whiskey wasn't in me, the stars would be too far away, and it would seem a foolish thing to try. If you had me, I'd wreck us both."

She still didn't say anything and the wind kept blowing.

"I can talk," I went on, "and I can walk the earth and make up funny little sayings and eat properly with a knife and fork and wear a double-breasted coat, but I couldn't make you happy. I could love you until the night was gone and we'd both burn with it, but in the day my lack of wholeness would be startling, and you'd want a butcher or baker . . ."

She turned and put her hands on the lapel of my coat. Her eyes were bright and her voice was angry. "How do you know what I want?" she asked hurriedly, fiercely. "Who gave you the right to decide for me?"

I bit my lips. She didn't understand.

"What I'm trying to tell you is that I'm as phoney as a one dollar alarm clock, that I don't like myself, and that every time I kissed you I was thinking about something else."

They were nice phrases. I decided that I hadn't done much better. Certainly my audience had never been more intense. She stood there with my lapel clutched in her hands, and she began to cry. Not with sorrow, but with vexation. The fury of it shook her slender shoulders and moved her breasts.

"But you love me," she accused angrily.

"Yes," I said, "I think I love you."

She cried harder than ever, and shook me so that I was turned halfway around. Suddenly she let go and stepped back. My lapel was crumpled where she had held it. She was before me, lovely and fragile in the darkness.

"You fool," she whispered. "You blind stupid fool!"

And then she turned, with her hands up to her face, and went around the corner toward the dance floor. I wanted to call out, to tell her that I was right, that I knew. But there was only emptiness around me, and I didn't get to ask her to wear the yellow dirndl for me once in awhile. The thought came that if I was a respectful man, I would cry some, but it was not in me and I went down the stairs and walked across the golf course toward my house. No tears were in me, but something tight and sickening had me by the throat as I stumbled across the dark fairways.

24

IT WAS late in the afternoon, and Fred and I were sitting in the back of the car, waiting. We had been drinking steadily since morning, and had arrived at that state of tremendous dignity. A young boy named Jenkins was driving us, and he sat twisted around on the front seat. He could not have been over seventeen and he got on my nerves badly, but we needed someone to drive. The kid obviously thought he was in the fast set, and he took occasional and infinitesimal nips with a great air of bravado. He worried me, and two or three times I had started to tell him that the bright gonfalons of excitement he was seeking were not to be found in the bottle, that what it held was a fire that burned but did not warm truly, a fire that required constant replenishing. I knew that I ought to explain to him that there was a point you could reach where you weren't any good without it, and then a little farther along, another point where you weren't any good even with it. I knew I ought to tell him, but I didn't.

We had been sitting there for over an hour. Two days before, Jarvis had given us a last careless wave of his hand, and gone to California. At the last minute, I had handed him a quart of Canadian Club and wished him luck among the celebrities. His even teeth were all showing as he took the bottle and turned it over in his hands.

"You'll hear from me," he had said. "Just consult your local newspapers."

It was his exit line from Texas, and he stood motionless on the observation platform as the train chuffed out of the station. Fred and I had watched until he was out of sight, and then we had repaired to a convenient tavern. There, in the coolness of a booth, we had hoisted drinks and mused on the scattering of the flock. So grieved had we become that the next two days slipped by wraithlike. They had brought us to the car parked before the church.

My bags were down in the bottom of the car, and I had already said goodbye to my family, who thought I had left the day before. But I hadn't because Lucille was getting married two hundred feet away from us. That was why we were waiting.

We kept watching and drinking, and finally she came running out. Harold had her by the hand, and they broke from the side door of the church. She was in front, and her head was thrown back. One hand held the white satin folds of her dress, and she was laughing. There was a warm look about her, and her body moving under the long wedding gown smashed into my eyes and flexed the pupils to hard knots. It was desire, and something else. Desire for the lithe body I had put my hands and weight upon, and another thing for her face and personality, the difference in her. Cheap nostalgia, perhaps; it comes easily to drunks. A car was waiting for the happy couple, and when they had crossed the street and jumped in, it pulled away swiftly.

I took a drink and told Jenkins to go to Massara's. Bradley didn't say anything while we were going there, and we rolled along wrapped in our cocoon of artificial warmth.

We got a table at Massara's, and after awhile Joe, the proprietor, came over to talk to us. He was a big man with gnarled hands and a moon face. Hard eyes were dropped into the softness of his face, and a diamond ring glittered on his right hand.

"Understand you're leaving us?" he asked pleasantly, his hand on my shoulder.

"Yes." I didn't look up, and Fred invited him to sit down and have a drink. He eased into a chair.

"I'll have one with you," he said, "and then you have one with me."

"That sounds fair enough," laughed Bradley, and we did it, but our whiskey was a lot better than his. Jenkins gagged over it, and stumbled away toward the toilet.

"He's got to learn," said Massara generously. "Everybody's got to learn. . . ."

But I couldn't see it.

"Why," I asked, "does everybody have to learn?"

The big man shrugged his shoulders, but I couldn't interpret that. Jenkins came back from the toilet looking pale, and we drank along and talked about nothing. It is an exhaustive subject. Finally Fred got up to go after his date, and Jenkins went with him. Massara and I sat there, not talking at all, and soon he got up and turned on the lights. The place began to fill, and the music box began to boom out its syrupy lamentations. People got up from tables around me and started dancing, but I didn't notice them. They were only blurs that passed back and forth before my eyes, because I was on a honeymoon and not liking it very much.

When Fred came back, he had the Perrys, James Menshew, Ann Alice Wiggins, and another girl with him. They also had two quarts of whiskey, and in this I was interested. Menshew was a finance company collector going bald, and after two drinks, he wanted to talk about life. So, as they drank the whiskey, they all talked about life, and what they didn't know about it was a caution. Nancy Perry looked young and graceful, but the other two girls were not so good. Bradley's Ann Alice was quite large in the hips and somewhat bovine in appearance. She came of a good family, but was considered intemperate, and after a time had passed, she began to kiss Fred. They were enthusiastic kisses complete with sucking noises, and rather sickening to behold. Menshew's date was a thin cipher of a girl with grotesquely large breasts. She looked as if she had been fondled overmuch, and from Menshew's attentiveness I could not see that the fondling was to be halted abruptly.

When the gaiety was at its height, about midnight, Menshew got up from his chair.

"Attention!" he shouted, weaving on his feet. "I have an announcement to make."

Massara came over and cut down on the volume of the music box, those at the tables quieted appreciably, and the long line of blank backs at the bar turned around and became listening people. Menshew waved his arms for even greater quiet, and when it came, he put his right hand down on his date's shoulder. She looked up, startled.

"This girl," he said in a ringing voice, "has got the finest tail in Texas."

Then he sat down.

For a full ten seconds, silence hung in the place. People were caught with their heads cocked to one side, or holding a glass aloft, and they remained that way. We looked at Menshew with one accord, but he was calmly mixing a drink. Perry started shaking with laughter, and then it spread like a swift infection over the room, until it was a raucous roaring. Bradley slapped his head in amazement.

"Am I going crazy," he asked us generally, "or did he say what I thought he said?"

Perry was still whooping and Nancy was smiling slightly. The girl of whom Menshew had spoken so highly looked around with a slightly surprised mien, as though we should have known it all along. Comprehension came to her slowly, but when it did, she caught Menshew with a right hook that lifted him over backward in his chair. Glasses followed him to the floor and shattered, and he got up picking sharp fragments from his hands and looking at her reproachfully, but that was all. The men turned back toward the bar, and a hum of conversation welled up.

I was going unsteadily to the back a few minutes later when Fred stopped me. He was standing behind a pillar next to our table, and his broad face was working with rage.

"Massara's on the make for Ann," he said slowly. "I'll kill him if he touches her."

"How do you know?" I asked. Massara was big and mean.

"He stopped her the first time she came back here," said Fred, pointing to the women's toilet. He was breathing heavily, and he led me into a little room off the corridor. He kept the door open a trifle, and I stood close behind him.

After we had waited for a few minutes, Ann Alice came into the hallway, and Massara was behind her. He shut the door carefully, and kissed her hard, carelessly, pressed her back against the wall with his big body. We couldn't see anything but her head, hung at an angle in his arm, but abandon had loosened her. Bradley shifted in front of me as she opened her mouth to kiss Massara again. Then, while we watched, they whispered shortly and went to the end of the hall and up the stairs. Ann Alice was leaning against the big man, clutching his arm.

When they were out of sight, I followed Fred down the hall. A light was shining in the center room when we got to the top of the stairs, and we skirted around it. The rug was silent beneath us, and the door between the two rooms was halfway open. We went up to stand behind it, and through the thin crack of light we could see them both, and hear her drunken laughter. She was sitting at a table in the center of the room, and Massara had his coat off. As we watched, he picked her up and stalked across the room with amazing lightness. She was still laughing, but when he put her down and covered her, she said "no!" in a slurred voice.

Massara's bulk had her pinned to the couch, and his meaty hands were moving over her. His back was to us, but we could gauge their movement by the spasmodic shiftings of his elbows. She lurched vainly under him, and cried out again, but one of his hands went up to cover her mouth. It was the hand with the ring on it, and the big diamond winked brightly as she bit at his fingers. I swayed forward, but Fred stopped me with one outflung hand, and I looked at him, startled. His mouth was twisted, and the light came through the crack of the door and fell across his bumpy face.

Inside the other room, Massara gradually snaked up and blotted the girl from our sight. His hand was gone from her mouth, and she was whimpering softly, a strange prickling sound in the quietness. I felt sick deep down in the guts, and turned away. Bradley was partially crouching, watching them through the crack, and his lips were wet and shining where he had licked them. I stepped back into the darkness and lighted a cigarette. Fred didn't turn around when the match scraped, but I didn't give a damn anyway. Massara's great bulk labored on; I could hear him grunting, and then he started to get up, but her voice came sopping in to us through the stillness.

"Don't go," she whimpered, "don't go yet. . . ."

I turned around and walked back down the stairs. Fred was following me. It wasn't as easy as it might have been because the stairs were tricky, and had a habit of shifting beneath the feet. When we were back at the table, I took another drink and let it settle. It was the extra one, the one that Jarvis said made the big difference. Menshew was staring at me as I got up and put on my hat.

"Well," I said, "I think I'll go to Chicago."

They all said goodbye as cordially as they could, which was not much, and Bradley got his hat and came over to stand beside me. I could hear him breathing.

"How long will you be gone?" asked Menshew, fingering his bald spot.

"About twenty years," I answered.

"Okay." He waved his hands in dismissal. "See you in twenty years," and Fred and I went out the door and got in the car.

We passed a clock, and as well as I could make it out, I had four minutes left. I rolled the window down and let the cold air wash across my face.

"Fred," I said slowly, "I wouldn't do anything about it. It's just not worth it."

He made no answer, and I gave up. When we had parked, I got a redcap to take my bags, and Fred and I paced through the station. The train was about to leave, and a strident voice was calling out the fact.

"All aboard," the Voice cried, and I held out my hand to Bradley. He shook it, and I got on the train. On the steps, I turned for another look. He was still standing there, and he waved his hand again. Inside, I found my seat and sat down in it. Most of the berths were already made, and a porter came up and asked me if I wanted mine made. I told him thickly that I didn't want it yet, and he vanished noiselessly. A newspaper was in my pocket; I didn't remember how it had gotten there, but, by the side light, I tried to read it. All I could make out was the one word, "War," and I knew that was a lie. I was very scornful of it, for it wasn't really war. War wasn't a word in a headline. The green curtains that enclosed the other sleeping passengers wavered slowly with the movement of the train, and lights flowed by outside the window. Once the lonesome wail of the train's whistle sounded up ahead, but I didn't care. I was drunk and riding through the night. I didn't try to hold the swiftly rolling cars back, and I didn't lean forward in my seat and try to push them to a greater speed. I just sat there and rode along, hoping that I had caught the right train.

Acknowledgments

The author's family would like to express its sincere thanks to all who made this remarkable reprinting of Philip Atlee's most important novel, *The Inheritors*, possible:

James Donovan, friend, literary agent, guiding light, and genuine inspiration to accomplish the seemingly impossible. Your counsel is always priceless, prescient, and on the mark; your professionalism and good humor always admired and appreciated. With this new publication of *The Inheritors* you have now ushered twenty-five of Philip Atlee's books back into the world, a tremendous achievement by any measure. The entire Phillips Family, past, present, and future owes you a debt of profound and eternal gratitude—thank you!

Shawn Phillips, Number One Son, for his patience, insight, and his singular perspective. Jim Phillips is looking down on you in proud appreciation for your incredible career and accomplishments. May all the health, love, and clarity you have wished on others return to you tenfold.

Lisa and Atlee Phillips, without whom all of these efforts would lack meaning and purpose. Thank you for carrying on the Family legacy with such class and grace.

Beth Phillips, for all of the years of unerring percipience. No one else has your intuition for the future and understanding of the past history of the Phillips Family and how and why every person, place, event, and thing are interconnected.

E. R. Bills, whom, though of brief acquaintance, has proved to be not only the unexpected and critical key to both Philip Atlee's rediscovery as a legitimate author of merit, but the catalyst for this long-overdue reprint of *The Inheritors*. Our sincere gratitude and respect for your Texas tenacity and all the uncountable hours and days of hard work. Thank you.

Last, but never least, a heartfelt thanks to the amazing team at TCU Press for their patience and professionalism, including, but not limited to: Dan Williams, Marco Roc, Adrienne Martinez, and Paige Gulley.

About the Author

James Young Phillips (1915–1991), pseudonym Philip Atlee, was a Fort Worth native whose first novel so scandalized the well-to-do citizens of his hometown that it was banned from public library shelves. Following stints as a flight dispatcher, Marine, Broadway publicist, and screenwriter, he turned to writing mystery and espionage novels, ultimately selling millions of copies worldwide.

www.ingramcontent.com/pod-product-compliance
Lightning Source LLC
LaVergne TN
LVHW100922110826
845155LV00036B/48

9780875659695